He wouldn't ░░░░░░ **n't for Henrie** ░░░░░ **en he arrived** ░░░░

Not because she'd persuaded him to play cricket again, but because getting to know her had changed his life. Made him want a new start. He wished she could be there.

When he looked up she was standing on the boundary, holding Mollie by the hand, and he had to look again to make sure he wasn't seeing things. Then he was striding across to them, smiling his pleasure. 'You're the last two people I was expecting to see here.'

'It will be wonderful watching you get back into village life again,' she said softly.

He reached out and traced his fingers gently across her cheek. 'We both know who we have to thank for that, don't we?'

They were calling him, and as he walked to the crease everyone present—players, spectators, and those preparing the food—began to clap. It went on for some minutes, until someone shouted, 'Welcome back, Doc.' He raised his bat in salute and the game began.

Abigail Gordon loves to write about the fascinating combination of medicine and romance from her home in a Cheshire village. She is active in local affairs, and is even called upon to write the script for the annual village pantomime! Her eldest son is a hospital manager and helps with all her medical research. As part of a close-knit family, she treasures having two of her sons living close by, and the third one not too far away. This also gives her the added pleasure of being able to watch her delightful grandchildren growing up.

Recent titles by the same author:

THE VILLAGE DOCTOR'S MARRIAGE
COMING BACK FOR HIS BRIDE
A FRENCH DOCTOR AT ABBEYFIELDS
HER SURGEON BOSS

CITY DOCTOR, COUNTRY BRIDE

BY
ABIGAIL GORDON

All the characters in this book have no existence outside the imagination of the author, and have no relation whatsoever to anyone bearing the same name or names. They are not even distantly inspired by any individual known or unknown to the author, and all the incidents are pure invention.

First published in Great Britain 2007
Harlequin Mills & Boon Limited,
Eton House, 18-24 Paradise Road, Richmond, Surrey TW9 1SR

© Abigail Gordon 2007

ISBN-13: 978 0 263 85232 5
ISBN-10:   0 263 85232 6

Set in Times Roman 10½ on 13¼ pt
03-0407-48389

Printed and bound in Spain
by Litografia Rosés, S.A., Barcelona

CITY DOCTOR, COUNTRY BRIDE

CHAPTER ONE

THE Cheshire countryside was just as beautiful as she remembered it from her last visit, Henrietta thought as she drove down the steep brow to where the river flowed endlessly through the village, and it was about to take her into its fold.

She loved the place and the thought of being part of its rural community for the next few months was like balm to her bruised heart. The air was clean, the pace of life slower, and people smiled at each other. Most of them had lived there all their lives and for those who hadn't there was always a delightful settling in process.

Village life was far removed from working in Manchester, where she was employed as a locum in a busy general practice. Facing up to crowded waiting rooms, and visiting patients in tower blocks, pokey back streets and smart residential suburbs, before going back to an empty flat.

Yet she'd been happy enough in her urban surroundings. The days had flown with the demands of an endless number of patients and there had been Miles.

When her older sister had phoned to ask if she would pull up sticks and move into her house in the Cheshire countryside to look after her children for the next few months while she accompanied her husband on a diplomatic posting, Henrietta had been taken aback.

'I'd love to, Pamela,' she'd told her. 'But I do have to earn a living, you know. I love Mollie and Keiran, and if it had been two weeks, instead of a matter of months, I wouldn't hesitate.'

'You could change jobs.' Pamela had said, not to be put off.

'Oh, yes?' she'd commented dryly. 'And how would I do that?'

'There's a vacancy for a locum at the village practice. They're going to need some extra help over the next few months too. With regard to ourselves we don't want to take the children out of school before they break up in July. Then we'll be coming back for them and settling in Scandinavia for the forseeable future.'

As she'd listened, Henrietta had a vision of stone cottages with flower filled gardens nestling at the foot of the peaks and an easy-flowing river that housed herons and kingfishers along its banks. She'd also had a vision of a life without Mollie and Keiran, the nephew and niece that she adored. If they were going to be living abroad she would see little of them. So having them to herself for a while would be a pleasure too precious to pass by.

'Let me think about it,' she said.

'All right, but don't be too long,' urged Pamela. 'We are due to leave in a six weeks. I have to sort something out for the children and I won't be easy in my mind until I have. It would also be nice for Charles and I to have some time on our own.'

There was silence at the other end of the line, and Pamela said, 'Henny, you haven't seemed very happy recently. You don't have to tell me what's going on, but maybe a change could be good for you as well.'

Henrietta grimaced. Pamela had no idea what went on in her private life, but it was clear she'd picked up on something during the occasional telephone chats they'd had. 'And how do the children feel about you leaving them behind,' she asked. Steering away from the topic.

'They'll be fine if they're with you, Henny. You know how much they love you.' She adopted a wheedling tone, 'So shall I suss out this vacancy at the village practice, then?'

'You can suss it out, yes,' Henrietta said. 'But don't get your hopes up. There is nothing to say they'll take me on if I apply for it.'

That had been the beginning of it and what was happening today was the result, she thought as the road levelled out and she found herself driving beside the river.

She hadn't slept the night after Pamela's phone call. As she'd tossed and turned it had been as if the village had been reaching out to her. She'd stayed with her sister and her husband a few times when she'd had a free weekend. Pamela was the only family she had, and each time she'd fallen more under the spell of the place. There was also another reason why her sister's suggestion had been tempting.

It was connected with one of those things that Pamela assumed she didn't have...a relationship. She desperately needed a change of scene. It had come at just the right moment.

* * *

She'd got to know Miles Somerby because he'd had an apartment just across the hall from hers and they had often passed each other, going in and out. He was of a similar age to herself, pleasant, not unattractive, with a rather reserved manner that she'd responded to.

As their acquaintance had progressed, Henrietta had thought that maybe here was the man she wanted to marry. Someone who would give her children and a happy family life. He'd made no secret of the fact that he was keen to see more of her and everything had been fine, until one day his ex-wife had knocked on her door and warned her that he was the father of a four-year-old boy that he never took the time to take out or visit.

'Miles can see our child whenever he wants,' she'd told a dumbstruck Henrietta. 'Georgie is always asking where his daddy is, but Miles can't be bothered to come and see him. If you've got something serious going with him, don't bank on him being a family man.'

When she'd gone Henrietta had crumbled beneath the hurt of what she'd just heard. Miles hadn't told her he'd been married before and that he had a child. She loved children, would want some of her own, and *he* couldn't even be bothered to go and see his.

She'd tackled him about it. First for not telling her he'd been married before, and he'd told her he hadn't thought it necessary. That had been hurtful enough, but when she'd brought up the matter of his little boy, the hurt had gone much deeper.

'I'm not really into kids,' he'd said with a shrug.

'But you know that I am, don't you? And you never

said,' she'd flung back at him. 'Your ex-wife has done me a favour. We're finished, Miles. You having been married before I could have coped with if you'd told me, but your attitude towards your son is unbelievable. I feel I've had a lucky escape.'

When he'd gone she'd cried, not so much for her hopes and dreams, but because of his deceit. How could any man not want to see his child and not feel it necessary to inform her of the little one's existence. It had left an aching void in her life. Made her wary of other relationships, and that had been how it had been when Pamela had got in touch.

Looking after her nephew and niece would be the icing on the cake if she agreed to do what Pamela wanted, she'd thought during the long hours of that night. Also it would be something to remember them by once they'd moved abroad.

Her sister knew that Mollie and Keiran would be safe with her until she and Charles came back and it would avoid them having to leave their school before the end of the school year.

The next day when Pamela had phoned to say that she'd got details of the position at the village practice, Henrietta had asked her to send them to her and it had all moved on from there.

In the month before Pamela and Charles had been due to leave she'd been interviewed for the vacancy along with other applicants, and had then sat back and waited.

'If I don't get the job you'll have to have a rethink,' she'd told Pamela. 'I'm not prepared to give up my present position until I know I have something to move to.'

'You'll get it,' her sister had said confidently, and Henrietta had wished that life would treat her as kindly as it did her sister. She had a loving husband on a fantastic salary. Two children who were dear to Henrietta's own heart, even though pressure of work meant that she didn't see them as often as she would have liked. Pamela also had a figure that curved in all the right places, which made *her* feel like a stick insect, when in truth she was a slender, fine-boned, twenty-nine-year-old with hazel eyes and dark brown hair.

She had been interviewed by a pleasant, middle-aged GP, who had explained that he was having to move south for a while to be near his elderly parents, and that the senior partner who had gone out to give medical aid after an earthquake in Pakistan, had asked him to find a replacement, so that he wouldn't come back to a practice without a doctor.

'When Matthew Cazalet left for Pakistan neither he nor I had cause to expect I would be caught up in a family crisis that would mean me being absent for some time,' John Lomas had said. 'I'm going to try and hang on until he gets back, and. if I can't, whoever I appoint will just have to do the best they can until his return.'

She hadn't liked the sound of that one bit and if it hadn't been for the joyous welcome she'd received that day from Mollie and Keiran when she'd turned up for the interview, she might have had second thoughts about the job side of the arrangements.

At that time he hadn't made any decisions, but she'd known if she was offered the position she wouldn't be able to refuse for the children's sake and for her own. She needed the tranquillity of the countryside to take away the hurt that Miles had caused. She'd put on a cheerful face for Pamela and her family but deep inside she had been feeling lost and lonely.

A few days later she'd been offered the position and from then on Henrietta had felt as if she was on a roller-coaster. There'd been her notice to give in at the city practice, the flat to rent out, and a host of other things to do in connection with moving house, but now, at last, she had arrived in the place where she'd longed to be.

The property where her sister and brother-in-law lived was called The White House and it had everything but the American president installed behind its impressive white portals. Smooth green lawns surrounded the house, and its interior was so expensively furnished Henrietta always felt a touch uncomfortable inside it. But, like it or not, it was going to be her home for some time to come.

As she drove through large ornate gates at the entrance to a winding driveway, she was telling herself that she was going to have to get used to it. That she wasn't there just for the weekend this time.

Since being offered the position at the practice she'd had a further conversation with John Lomas, and been told that the senior partner was still in Pakistan, but should be back soon. With regards to himself he'd said that he hoped to be there to show her the ropes but might have to leave soon afterwards.

'It's been rather chaotic since Matthew went,' he'd told her. 'Coping without him, and then my mother having a serious stroke, which is why I'm moving south for a while to be near her. But once he's back in charge again I'm sure you'll find a rural practice a pleasant change from urban health care.'

'I hope so,' she'd told him doubtfully at the thought of being caught up between one doctor's departure and another's return.

And now the time had come to take on the two new roles that she'd let herself be talked into—childminder and country doctor—and she had a feeling that the first was going to be the easiest.

When she pulled up in front of the house in her modest car Pamela came out to greet her and as they hugged each other her sister said, 'I've prepared the largest guest room for you, Henny. Had it decorated, the drapes cleaned and new carpeting fitted.'

'You didn't have to,' she protested as they stood in the doorway of a bedroom that was as big as the whole of the flat she'd just left. 'I'm not used to a life of luxury.'

'So now is your chance,' she was told. 'The children's rooms are on each side of you. They didn't want to go to school this morning when they knew you were coming, but I reminded them that this isn't your usual hasty visit. That they'll be seeing a lot of you…and you of them.'

Henrietta smiled. Six-year-old Mollie, who had her mother's fair colouring, and Keiran, a year older with a mop of russet curls, were the least of her worries when it came to looking after them. It was the responsibility that went with it that she was concerned about. Just as she was apprehensive at the thought of becoming a member of a practice that seemed to be short on doctors.

She was hoping that John Lomas would still be there when she reported for duty on the following Monday. As for his absent partner, she would cross the hurdle of meeting him when she came to it.

Whatever he turned out to be like she had to hand it to him for taking his skills to the land so badly damaged by an earthquake. She wondered how long he'd been out there and what his family thought about it, presuming that he was married.

There was the sound of running feet on the fine gravel of the driveway outside and the high pitch of children's voices. Mollie and Keiran had just been dropped off by the mother of a child who went to the same school, and as they flung themselves into her arms Henrietta felt tears prick.

Not so long ago she'd thought that she was moving towards family life. That she'd met the man who would father *her* children. Only to discover that he'd already been there, done it, then shaken off the shackles in the divorce court.

'What's this Matthew Cazalet person like?' she enquired of her sister over dinner that evening. 'I believe he's in Pakistan, helping out after an earthquake.'

'Yes, so I'm told,' Pamela replied. 'I'm afraid that I don't know much about him as we have private health care. I invited him to a dinner party once but he made the excuse that he was too busy.'

'In other words, our local doctor is not one of Pamela's conquests,' her husband said with an affectionate smile. 'She likes to feel that under her mantle of lady of the manor she has them all docketed and filed, but not so Matthew Cazalet.'

'Nonsense, Charles,' Pamela protested. 'When I invited him to my dinner party I was hoping to do a little matchmaking.'

'Not with Cazalet!' he hooted. 'If ever there was a man capable of organising his own life, it's him.'

It was time to change the subject, Henrietta thought. The more she heard about the man who was to be her new boss, the more she was thinking that the job part of her move into the countryside didn't sound like a piece of cake.

For one thing she was going to have to get used to the more personal nature of village health care. In her last job, the people she'd come across had been mainly just sick bodies and faces that had soon been forgotten. Except for Miles, who was still living in the flat across the hall from hers.

It was Monday morning. Pamela and Charles had departed on the Saturday and Henrietta and the children had made the most of a wonderfully sunny Sunday by swimming in the pool at the back of the house in the morning and taking a picnic up onto the moors in the afternoon.

Mollie and Keiran had loved that. Romping amongst the heather and bracken and shouting excitedly when a sheep had trotted past. There were just a few properties up there, the odd cottage and one or two remote farms, which she thought would be pleasant enough to visit in the summertime if someone needed a doctor, but might be seen in a different light in the snow, or when high winds blew.

But she might be gone before winter set in if the surgery

didn't need her any more and Pamela and Charles had come back to take the children to a new life.

As they had come chasing towards her, happy to be roaming free, she'd set out the picnic and told herself to make the most of what circumstances were offering.

The children went to school happily enough. Henrietta drove them down to the pick-up point for the special bus that would take them to the private school that they attended, and they'd skipped on board. The novelty of having their favourite aunt around the place had prevented any upset from waving their parents goodbye.

In the afternoon the housekeeper who came in each weekday would meet them from the bus and would stay with them until she, Henrietta, had finished at the surgery. It had all been arranged by their mother and she had yet to meet the lady who kept the house in order under her sister's watchful eye.

When she arrived at the surgery on the main street of the village, John Lomas was already there and looking tense. 'I really do hate having to do this, Dr Mason,' he said aplogeti-cally, 'but I am going to have to leave you in charge. My father has just phoned to say that my mother is gravely ill. Her condition has worsened overnight and I must go to her.'

He pointed to one of the receptionists smiling at her from behind the counter. 'Judy will show you the ropes and I've instructed all staff to give you every assistance. Matthew Cazalet is on his way home, but he hasn't shown up so far. So do you think you'll be all right taking the surgery this morning. I'm afraid that the waiting room is rather full.'

'It would seem that I have no choice,' Henrietta said wryly. 'I'd better gather my wits and get organised before it starts. I'm so sorry to hear about your mother. I lost mine some time ago and can imagine what you are going through. I do hope that you'll find her improved.'

He flashed her a grateful smile and was gone, leaving her to think that it was a bit much, the senior partner not being there. It was all very well doing his bit overseas, but this fellow Cazalet had a duty to his patients here and to herself.

'Does it matter which room I use?' she asked Judy.

'No. I don't suppose so,' was the reply. 'Both doctors are absent.' Judy gave her a sympathetic smile. 'You're in charge.'

Henrietta swallowed hard and settled herself behind the desk in the nearest of the two consulting rooms.

'I'll go and get the patient's notes,' Judy said, 'and then you'll be ready.'

'Yes, do that, but before you go, if I need to send a patient to see one of the practice nurses how many are on duty?'

'Two. Both poised for action,' Judy assured her.

'I'm glad that somebody is,' Henrietta told her with a wry smile.

Matthew Cazalet was tired. He'd been at the site of the earthquake a month and it had been hard. Very hard. No sooner had the team he'd been working with treated one of the injured homeless than there had been hundreds more begging for help.

He was back sooner than intended because of John's

family crisis. The last time they'd spoken the older man had still been holding the reins at the practice and had taken on another doctor to fill the gap that he was about to leave.

Before he did anything and, heaven only knew, he was longing for a shower and some food, he was going to call in at the surgery to make sure that everything was under control. But he didn't intend going in through the front door because he looked a sight.

The dark thatch of his hair needed cutting. There were deep creases beneath eyes that were red-rimmed through lack of sleep, and he desperately needed a shave. The last thing he wanted was for the villagers to see him in that state, so it was the back door through which he intended making his entrance.

He could hear raised voices in the reception area and recognised one of them as that of Gregory Hicks, a farmer who always caused friction when he attended the surgery. The other belonged to one of the receptionists. It was a heated argument that was taking place and he frowned. Where was John?

The door of his consulting room was ajar and he halted in his tracks when he saw the woman sitting behind his desk. He was too jaded to be bothered with the niceties and asked abruptly, 'So who might you be? Where's John, and this Henry fellow that he's taken into the practice? It's bedlam out there.'

Henrietta got slowly to her feet. This was the last straw, she thought wildly. If this was the prodigal doctor, he needed a lesson in manners…and hosing down!

'It must have been a bad line when you were talking

to your colleague,' she said, trying to keep calm. 'There is no Henry *fellow*. I am Henrietta Mason. It is my first day here and I'm having to cope on my own. Dr Lomas had to leave the moment I arrived as his mother has taken a turn for the worse.

'I was told that you—I'm presuming that you are Matthew Cazalet, as you haven't introduced yourself—were somewhere between here and Pakistan. A situation that has not made my introduction to rural medicine one of the highlights of my life. Regarding the racket that was going on in Reception, it seems to have quietened down. I was about to go and see what the problem was when you appeared.'

'I'm sorry,' he said flatly. 'It's just that you were a surprise. I sneaked in the back way because I don't want my patients to see me until I've recharged my batteries. But I had to stop off to make sure that all was in order here.'

'And now you find that it's not.'

He didn't reply to that. 'I'll be back the moment I've showered and changed my clothes, and then we'll talk. I take it that you've managed to cope with morning surgery.'

'Yes.'

She wasn't going to tell him that it had been a doddle compared to what she'd been used to, and if it hadn't been for the row in the passage he would have arrived to find all in order, plus an empty waiting room. 'I was just about to start doing the home visits in an area that I'm not at all familiar with, so your arrival is opportune, to say the least.'

Henrietta hid a smile as she watched his jaw tighten. She could tell he was used to being in charge. So she wasn't going to tell him that she'd done hundreds of home visits in strange places without batting an eyelid in her previous job. It went with urban living.

'Don't start them until I get back,' he said tightly. 'Unless there is anything urgent.'

She nodded. 'Whatever you say. I'll be having a look through them while I'm waiting.'

'Yes, do that,' he said, still with no warmth in his voice. 'I won't be long.'

Matthew had asked the taxi driver who'd brought him from the airport to wait outside the surgery and now, as he was driven to the house where he'd lived alone since losing Joanna, he was facing up to the fact that he wasn't going to be throwing himself into bed once he'd showered. He'd been expecting to find John in control and Dr Henry Mason filling in, only to discover that John was gone and Henry was Henrietta.

The leggy woman with the long brown hair had made it clear that she took a dim view of the way she'd found herself thrown in at the deep end and he understood her annoyance. She had arrived to find herself piggy in the 'muddle', he thought with grim humour. Once he was back in charge any chaos would level out and the practice would be what it had always been—an efficiently run centre of health care.

When the taxi driver stopped outside his own house, a bleak-looking semi-detached built from local limestone, he thought, as he'd often done before, that it was time he stopped mourning Joanna. Nothing was going to bring her back.

He'd known the moment he'd seen her lying at the foot

of a steep drop below one of the peaks that she was gone from him without any farewells. She'd been out with the rambling club from the village and when a teenage lad had been showing off and fallen over the edge of the drop she'd reached down to pull him back up again off the bush that he'd landed on. But in his fear he'd grabbed at her to pull himself to safety, causing her to lose her balance, and she'd gone hurtling down onto rocks below.

It had been three years ago and he'd proved wrong the saying that time healed all wounds. He still missed her terribly and every time he thought about all the plans for the future they'd had, plans that had included starting a family, it was like a knife turning in his heart.

He smiled when he went into the tidy kitchen. There was a note on the table that read, 'Did a big bake yesterday. Your freezer is full for when you come home. I've missed you, Matthew. Love, Aunt Kate.'

Kate Crosby was his mother's younger sister. She'd brought him up after his mother had died when he'd been twelve and his father had remarried and gone to live abroad, and after he'd lost Joanna she'd stepped back into the role that had been hers during his early teens, until he'd gone to study medicine.

She was a strong, sturdy woman, with boundless energy, some of which she spread around as daily housekeeper to the wealthiest family in the village.

He didn't know Pamela and Charles Wainwright very well as they didn't belong to the practice, but he heard about them from Kate and once they'd invited him to a dinner party. It had been shortly after Joanna's death and the last thing he'd wanted had been to be pitied or put on show as an eligible widower, so he had politely refused.

As he put Kate's note back on to the kitchen table he caught a glimpse of himself in the mirror in the hall and gave a grim smile. It was a wonder that the indignant Henrietta hadn't called for help when such an unsavoury looking character had appeared.

In recent weeks there had been no time for smart haircuts and shaving, and, more importantly, little time for sleeping and eating. The needs of those he'd met had been endless. Yet in a strange sort of way he'd been happier out there than at any time since he'd lost his wife.

He was back at the practice within the hour, scrubbed clean, shaved, dressed in clean clothes and munching on a huge barm cake filled with cheese and ham.

Henrietta almost smiled when she saw him. Matthew Cazalet had looked exhausted when he'd appeared out of the blue, but it would seem that he was resilient enough when he had to be.

Was he married? she wondered. Had he got a caring wife who'd made him the sandwich and had then had to sit back and watch him dash off again the moment he'd arrived home?

But there was work to be done and the private life of the man who'd perched himself on the corner of the desk while he wolfed down the sandwich was of no interest to her whatsoever.

'One of the home visits *was* urgent,' she told him. 'So I went out on it while I was waiting.'

Dark brows were lifting. She was a cool customer, this one.

'Really? Who was it you went to see?'

'An old fellow in a remote cottage set amongst fields. There were dead foxes hanging from his garden wall.'

'That would be Jack Yardley,' he said immediately. 'He's obsessed with pest control. And so what ails him? He's a tough old rascal. We don't often see him down here.'

She smiled and he thought that her eyes were her best feature. They were dark hazel with long lashes and there was a directness in her glance that might have appealed to him if he hadn't been on the receiving end of her disenchantment.

'That has changed, I'm afraid. He's in with the nurse now. Jack has got a badly infected hand. Gashed it on some barbed wire and hasn't been looking after it as he should. I've put him on a course of antibiotics and am hoping that those and the nurse's attentions might prevent it going septic.'

Matthew nodded. 'That sounds fine. He's a strange old guy. Almost a hermit.' He was seating himself in the chair behind his desk, which she had tactfully left vacant.

'So tell me about yourself. Where were you working previously, and are you living locally?'

'I've been working as a locum at a large practice in the city centre.'

'What made you leave?'

'My sister, who lives in the village, asked me to look after her children for a few months while she went with her husband on a diplomatic posting. He's a civil servant in the Foreign Office.'

He was observing her incredulously. 'Are you telling me that you are related to the Wainwrights?'

'Yes. Pamela is my older sister.'

'I see,' he said slowly. 'And you had to change jobs to do what she asked?'

'Yes, but I didn't mind. I've always envied Pam and her husband living in a place like this, and I'm very fond of Mollie and Keiran. Looking after them will be a pleasure. It's the rest of it I'm not sure about.'

'I take it that you are referring to this practice. I intend to reassure you about that. I didn't go out to Pakistan as a tourist, you know, and while I was there didn't spend the time twiddling my thumbs. I saw a great need and tried to do my bit, leaving the practice in John's capable hands.'

'Yes, I know.' She nodded. 'It must have been a nightmare out there.'

'It still is, but at least I've done a little to help, and I'm sorry if I was ratty when I arrived. The last thing I expected was to find a stranger in charge, and Hicks throwing his weight about didn't help. Whatever it was, he soon went, so they must have sorted him out in Reception. I wouldn't have liked you to have that thrown at you as well on your first day.'

Then he gave her a quizzical smile, and Henrietta found herself smiling back. 'So, are we going to call a truce?'

'I don't have much choice, do I? I have to earn a living.'

She could have enlightened him further but didn't see why she should. Her personal life had nothing to do with this dark-haired doctor with the tired eyes and decisive manner. She was still feeling low after the breakdown of her affair with Miles and was in no mood to be confiding her affairs to anyone, least of all a stranger.

'Right, shall we start on the home visits?' he was saying. 'We'll do them together for a couple of days until you know the area better.'

Henrietta nodded. She was feeling less fraught now that some sort of order was being maintained, and wished that she hadn't been so snappy when they'd first met.

The man observing her from behind his desk may have not been Mr Charm himself, but going to Pakistan showed that he was a doctor through and through. And at that time he hadn't expected that the man he'd left in charge of the practice would have had to leave in such a hurry.

As they drove along the main street of the village towards their first call, Matthew was thinking that the woman beside him didn't fit in with the wealthy Wainwrights. Pamela was well meaning but patronising, and Charles went about with the smug expression of a man of importance.

He hadn't told Henrietta that his Aunt Kate was their housekeeper. He didn't know why, unless it was because he wished she wasn't. But Kate liked looking after the immaculate White House and if that was what gave her a buzz, it wasn't for him to interfere.

The woman sitting beside him would find out soon enough that he and Kate were related and probably be just as surprised as he'd been to know that she was Pamela Wainright's sister.

When he stopped the car in front of a wooden building on a large plot of land across the way from a small country railway station, Henrietta looked around her questioningly.

'This place used to be the cattle market in years gone by,' he explained 'but now the building is a café run by a young couple who have tried to keep the atmosphere, which you'll see when we go inside. They sold their house to buy it and have put every penny they possess into it. The result is that they're having to live in a caravan at the back of the premises. So let's go and see how Jackie Marsland is doing.'

When they went into the café Henrietta understood what he'd meant about keeping the atmosphere. The inside was divided up into alcoves similar to cattle stalls and there was clean straw on the floor. On the counter there were small milk churns full of home-made cookies and an array of wholesome-looking sandwiches.

Every table was occupied and when the young fellow behind the counter saw them he said, 'Dr Cazalet, Jackie is in the caravan. She's got severe stomach pains.'

'Come in,' a voice called weakly when Matthew knocked on the door. As the two doctors went inside Henrietta saw a woman of a similar age to herself lying on one of the bunk beds.

'So how long have you had stomach pains, Jackie?' Matthew asked as he bent over her.

'Since I got up this morning,' she told him.

'Any diarrhoea?'

'No. It's not like a gastric upset, Doctor. I'm twelve weeks pregnant and am scared that I might be losing the baby.'

'Are you bleeding?' he asked gravely.

'Yes, I am a bit.'

The young woman on the bed was looking at Henrietta.

'Who's this?' she asked, drawing her legs up as another stab of pain came.

'Dr Henrietta Mason,' he informed her. 'Would you like *her* to examine you?'

'I'm not bothered,' Jackie said. Tears threatened. 'I feel so guilty. We didn't want a family just yet. We simply can't afford it, so instead of being happy about my pregnancy we've been fed up, feeling that we have enough responsibility at present without more of it coming our way. But now that I might be going to have a miscarriage I'm ashamed of what I've been thinking.'

When he'd examined her Matthew said, 'OK, Jackie, we'll get you admitted to hospital and they'll take it from there.' His tone was gentle. 'And, please, try not to blame yourself. You won't be the only woman who's felt that way, so don't feel guilty about not being as happy about it as you might have been under other circumstances.'

He turned to Henrietta. 'Would you mind going to the café to tell Jackie's husband that we are having her admitted to hospital and then phoning for an ambulance?'

'Of course.' Henrietta smiled reassuringly at Jackie and headed for the café, impressed with Matthew's gentle handling of the distressed patient. Here was a doctor clearly devoted to the people in his care and, despite their rocky start earlier this morning in the surgery, it gave her hope for a good working relationship if nothing else.

CHAPTER TWO

DRIVING around the village and through the nearby country-side, Matthew could smell Henrietta's perfume in the warmth of the car and it was achingly familiar, so much so that he clenched his teeth in anguish.

It was the same one that Joanna had worn. He was sure of it, had smelt it often enough, and he wondered why this woman doctor, who was nothing out of the ordinary except for her eyes, was wearing an expensive perfume while on duty. It didn't go with the image.

'The perfume, what's it called?' he asked.

Henrietta swivelled in her seat and stared at him in amazement. He was a strange creature, this country GP, she thought. The last person she would have expected to ask such a question, but maybe he liked it and was considering buying some for a wife or woman friend. Or, then again, maybe he didn't like it.

'It's called Destination,' she said slowly. 'Why do you ask? If you are finding it unpleasant, please, say so.'

He shook his head. 'No. Nothing like that. It just seems a bit exotic for a doctor's surgery.'

It was a weak excuse and he knew it, but did he want to be reminded of the wife he'd lost all the time he was with Henrietta Mason? It would be just too painful.

'I get the message,' she said quietly, 'and won't wear it again for work. It was a gift last Christmas and I loved it from the moment I sprayed it on.'

'Yes, well, if you could keep it for out of working hours.'

'No problem,' she said equably. 'I'll keep the perfume strictly for socialising, not that I'm expecting to be doing much of that while I'm here.'

When they'd finished the home visits he said, 'What are you going to do about lunch? Go to your sister's place? Try the café we called at earlier? Or bring something back to eat? There's a baker's just across from the surgery and the lady who does the cleaning for us always has the kettle on the boil.'

'What do you usually do for lunch?' she asked.

'Grab a bite when I can. But today I'll have something to eat at the café. I want to tell Jackie Marsland's husband that I'll take over the café for him this evening so that he can go to visit her.

'The girl has no parents or other near relatives, and the place doesn't close until eightish. As you saw when we called, he was up to his eyes in it and will be frantic at not being with her at such a worrying time, but they just can't afford to lose any trade. Do you want to come and have your lunch there?'

'No. I'll go across the road for a sandwich,' she told him, feeling the need to gather her wits. Only hours before he had appeared at the surgery looking like death and now was offering to take over the café while its owner went to see his pregnant wife.

* * *

As he made his way to the brightly coloured wooden building that had been the old cattle market, Matthew was feeling guilty for having made such a fuss about the perfume. Henrietta wasn't to know that by wearing it she'd opened one of the pain valves in his heart, and now she was probably thinking that he was nit-picking in retaliation for the way she'd put him in his place when he'd come sneaking in through the back door of the surgery.

Today's happenings hadn't created the best of beginnings to their working relationship, but did it matter? As long as she was a good doctor and pulled her weight in the practice, he would have no complaints.

By the time the afternoon surgery was finished Matthew was ready for home. He'd been intending to catch up on some sleep when he'd called in at the surgery that morning, but after meeting the new doctor he could no more have slept off his tiredness than fly.

She'd taken him to task and though she'd seemed to approve of his sojourn abroad, Henrietta Mason was wary of him. He could feel it in her cool hazel glance.

At the second surgery of the day she'd seen all her patients long before he had, but there had been a reason for that. Almost every person he'd treated had wanted to hear about his time in Pakistan and to express their pleasure at his return. It had been gratifying but time-consuming, and when he arrived back home once more he went straight up to bed for a couple of hours and was asleep in seconds.

He awakened to the sound of Kate's voice beside him, and as he looked up at her drowsily she said, 'Welcome home, lad. I'll be able to sleep easy tonight, knowing that you're back.'

He smiled up at her. 'You're the best sight I've seen in days, Aunt Kate. In my weakest moments out there I thought of your steak and kidney puddings and hung on.'

'There's one steaming on the stove at this moment,' she told him briskly. 'It's ready for serving any time, and I've made a *crème brûlée*. They are your welcome home feast before you have to rush off to the café. Poor Jackie. I hope she'll be all right.'

As she put the food in front of him Kate said, 'Do you want me to bring you up to date with all the local news?'

'Such as the new doctor we've taken on at the practice being pushy Pamela's sister?' he said dryly.

'So you know?'

'Yes. I do. We've met and she's not impressed with me.'

'Why ever not?'

'Mainly because she turned up there this morning and found she was the only doctor present. John's mother has taken a turn for the worse and he was on his way to be with her, and yours truly was in transit from the airport. I sneaked in the back way, looking like a tramp, and found her at my desk, which didn't please me all that much. Then to cap it all I discovered her connection with the Wainwrights.'

'Yes. I met Henrietta late this afternoon,' Kate said. 'I've been asked to meet the school bus and stay with the children until she comes home from the surgery on weekdays. On first acquaintance I would say that she's nothing like her sister. She hasn't got Pamela's bounce and style, but the children adore her and she's lovely with them. So natural and friendly.'

'Are we talking about the same person?' he asked quizzically. 'Or was it just me getting off on the wrong foot with her?'

Henrietta had enjoyed meeting Kate Crosby, especially after she'd said, 'You're nothing like Pamela, are you?'

'No. I'm from the poor side of the family,' she'd told her laughingly. 'But I come in useful at times.'

'We wish that Henny lived here in the village so that we could see her all the time,' Mollie had said, and Keiran had nodded his agreement.

Now the children were in bed and so was she. But not to sleep. Her mind was too full of the day's events and uppermost were the moments she'd spent with Matthew Cazalet.

Kate had informed her that she was his aunt and Henrietta had been able to tell from her tone that she had a great affection for him, but that had been all she'd said about him. There had been no information about his private life and there was no way she was going to ask.

Her curiosity came from the circumstances of their meeting, she told herself, and wondered what tomorrow would bring at the village practice.

The children caught the school bus at eight o'clock each morning, which gave Henrietta just enough time to drop them off before making her way to the surgery. Or at least it would have done if Keiran hadn't forgotten his homework.

After driving back to the house to get it and having to

chase the bus for a couple of miles before she caught up with it, she was ten minutes late for morning surgery.

Matthew had already started treating those who were waiting to see him by the time she arrived, so Henrietta scuttled quickly into the smaller of the two consulting rooms and, after making sure that the patient's notes were on her desk, called in the first one. Hoping that she looked cool and dignified and knowing she didn't.

She knew that Matthew's regulars would be keen to be treated by him, and that she would be dealing with the mish-mash of those who had made last-minute appointments, or just wanted to see any doctor.

That was how it had been at the late surgery the day before, but not so the previous morning when she'd arrived to find she had been the only doctor there and had had to deal with the lot of them.

Whether anyone had cancelled on finding that the two regular doctors were not available, she didn't know. But from now on she intended to make her presence felt, make a niche for herself in this country practice, and as one strange face followed another, she thought wryly that her late arrival had not been in keeping with that sort of thinking.

Tomorrow, before any of them set foot out of the house, she would make sure that the children had everything they needed for school. Today had been a lesson learned. Her expression softened at the thought of the two young ones who'd been placed in her care.

'So you're the new doctor,' an overweight, middle-aged man with high colour said when he'd settled himself across from her in the middle of the morning.

'Yes, I am. Mr…er…Warburton,' she said, referring to his notes. 'What can I do for you?'

He sighed. 'Not a lot, I should think. I've got diabetes and am on medication for it. I have to come in every so often for a check-up and that's why I'm here today.'

'I see, and how are you coping with it?'

'Terrible! I've always had a sweet tooth and if it wasn't for my wife keeping me on a strict diet, I'd be falling by the wayside.'

'I see from your notes that you're borderline. Have you tried to lose weight?'

'Yes. I'm on a low-fat diet.'

'What about exercise?'

'Not as often or as much as I should, I'm afraid.'

'Losing weight is a strange thing,' she told him. 'It takes a lot of willpower, but most people find that once it starts to go down the feeling is so gratifying that they become really keen to continue with it. But getting back to what you're here for. Surely you should be seeing the nurses in the diabetes clinic that they hold each Tuesday morning?'

He stared at her with hard blue eyes. 'Yes, I should, but as it's been cancelled and I wasn't informed. I've insisted on seeing you for my check-up. I live way up over the tops. It's a long way to come on a wasted journey.'

Henrietta groaned inwardly. She would have known that the clinic had been cancelled if she hadn't been late. It was to be hoped that this rather forthright individual wouldn't start complaining about having had further aggravation from the doctor.

'We'll start with your blood pressure, I think,' she said

calmly, 'and then I'll examine your feet, if you wouldn't mind taking off your socks and shoes.'

After she'd examined him and had taken blood and urine samples for testing, Fred Warburton got to his feet. 'Thank you, Doctor. I'd insist that you are kept informed of what's going on in this place, if I were you.'

'I'll bear that in mind,' she told him smoothly, and waited for him to depart.

'What happened?' Matthew asked when the surgery was over and they were having a quick coffee before starting the home visits. 'Yesterday I was the one who was missing and today it was your turn.'

He looked immaculate that morning she thought, in a smart suit, crisp white shirt and a subdued tie. He still needed a haircut but she knew there'd been no time for that since his return.

There'd been a gleam in his eye as he'd asked the question, and she knew he was thinking that the boot was on the other foot as he followed it up with, 'Did you oversleep?'

She shook her head. 'No. It was a hiccup that occurred while I was getting the children off to school. I drove them to where they pick up the school bus and as they were getting on Keiran remembered that he'd left his homework behind and threw a wobbler. So we had to go back and get it. When we'd done that we discovered that the bus had gone and I had to chase it for a couple of miles before we caught up. It won't happen again, I assure you. I shall be making absolutely sure they've got everything in future.'

He nodded. 'How old is Kieran?'

'Six.'

'Seems a bit young for homework. But having no children of my own, I'm not up to date with what goes on in the education system. You've taken on a big responsibility, looking after someone else's children night and day.'

'That doesn't bother me. I have no other agendas in my life at present, apart from working here, and with regard to that my being late meant that I didn't know the diabetes clinic had been cancelled. One of my patients took great pleasure in informing me of the fact and insisted on seeing a doctor instead. He said that he'd come a long way and didn't want to have to make a second journey, which I have to say I understood.'

'That would be Fred Warburton. The clinic was cancelled because we are short-staffed. One of the nurses is on holiday and another of them rang in sick this morning, which only left one to do everything. We tried to phone him but he'd already left.

'The fact that we have only one nurse today is also probably the reason why you weren't informed that the clinic had been cancelled. But one of the receptionists should have made sure you knew and I shall mention that to them. I expect you to be prompt and efficient, but am not demanding that you be psychic.'

'They probably didn't see me arrive. I didn't exactly sneak in by the back door,' she told him with a twinkle, 'but I nipped into my room smartish and they wouldn't have known I'd arrived until I started calling the patients in. So, you see, it *was* my fault that I didn't know.'

As they went out to his car Matthew was thinking that this

replacement in the practice was not prepared to see someone told off for a situation that she'd been responsible for. It would have been easy to let someone else take the blame.

As they fastened their seat belts he said, 'You mentioned your sister's children catching the school bus, so obviously they don't attend the one in the village.'

'No, they don't. Mollie and Keiran go to a private school somewhere on the borders of Derbyshire and Cheshire.'

He didn't say anything, just looked rather grim, and she saw that his glance was on a group of ramblers going past. Yet they weren't making a nuisance of themselves, far from it. They waved and called good morning and she waved back, but Matthew just nodded rather stiffly. He started the car and they moved off.

'Where do *you* live, Dr Cazalet?' she asked as they drove around the village. 'You know where I'm based, but I don't know the same thing about you. I met your aunt yesterday. Do you live with her?'

'No,' he said levelly. 'I live alone and, for goodness' sake, Henrietta, drop the Dr Cazalet. My name is Matthew.'

She was smiling, not prepared to be put off. 'So, Matthew, where do you live?'

'We'll be passing it in a moment. Not much to look at. My wife and I bought it when we were first married. We thought it had the potential to make a gracious home. But when I was left on my own the plans we'd made seemed pointless. Now it's just somewhere to sleep.'

Henrietta nodded absently. She was wondering if she dared ask him where his wife was and, as if he'd read her mind, he said flatly, 'My wife is dead.'

'Oh!' she exclaimed. 'I'm so sorry.'

'Yes, so am I,' he said as he slowed the car in front of his house, and wondered why on earth he was showing this woman he'd only just met where he lived.

'I hope you don't want a grand tour,' he said dryly as she gazed at the sombre stone building.

'No, of course not. I wouldn't dream of being so intrusive.'

'That's all right, then. Especially with you living in the palatial White House. A lot of folk will envy you that.'

'They don't need to,' she retorted as they moved off. 'I'm nervous in there. It's too big and sumptuous. I'm scared of putting a foot wrong. Before I came here I had a small flat. It was nothing special but it was my own. The whole of it would fit into the bedroom I'm using now, so you can tell how big it is.'

'And what have you done with it.'

'Rented it out. I had to. I need the money.'

'So your sister isn't funding the disruption she's caused in your life.'

'No. I wouldn't want her to. It's not necessary. Pamela would have been ready to offer if I'd given her the chance. But I had no intention of doing that. She's done me a favour. I've always envied her and Charles living here and it's one of the reasons I let her persuade me to fall in with her plans.'

'Yes, she does like people to fall in with her plans, doesn't she? But not everyone enjoys being manipulated. I certainly don't.'

She didn't know what that was supposed to mean and decided not to ask. This was a man who carried his grief around with him, felt things deeply. That would be one of the reasons why he'd gone to help the earthquake victims.

It wouldn't be hard to find out what had happened to his wife. She could ask Kate, or quiz Pamela when she next rang up to see how they were faring, but she wasn't going to do either of those things. Matthew would have to tell her himself if he wanted her to know.

'We had a call from Goyt Lodge while you were seeing the last of your patients,' he told her as they drove along the main street. 'It's a local guest house and it seems that someone staying there woke up this morning in a very confused state. From the details we were given, it seems that the lady had been perfectly all right the night before, but when she didn't come down to breakfast this morning the owner's wife went to check on her and found her wandering around the bedroom, not knowing who or where she was.'

'What age is she?' Henrietta asked.

'Sixties, I believe. You're thinking of Alzheimer's?'

'No, not really. Would we expect it to come on so suddenly? I was thinking more of a mini-stroke.'

'Maybe,' he agreed. 'Hopefully we'll soon find out.' He pointed to a solid-looking red brick building just off the road, 'That is Goyt Lodge. I've been called out to this place a couple of times before, but it's never been anything serious, so let's hope that this time turns out to be the same.'

They were shown into a small sitting room where a smartly dressed elderly woman was drinking tea out of a china cup, with a younger woman seated beside her.

The younger of the two women got to her feet when she

saw them, while the older one placed the cup noisily on to the saucer and asked, 'Who are these people, Lynda? They haven't come to take me away, have they?'

'No, of course not,' Lynda said. 'I sent for the doctor to come to see you as you aren't yourself this morning, are you?'

'That's true enough,' the elderly woman said as tears began to flow. 'I don't know who *myself* is and it's frightening.'

'What is the lady's name?' Matthew asked.

'Mrs Joan Carradine,' he was told. 'My husband and I own this place. She often stays here for a week or so. I believe she has friends in the area, but has never said who they are.'

'Have you noticed any problem with her movements?'

'No, none.'

'I'm just going to check you over,' Matthew told Mrs Carradine gently. 'There's no need to be alarmed. I'm going to sound your heart and feel your pulse to see if we can discover what has made you forgetful this morning.'

'All right,' the lady agreed, 'but *he* did it. He pushed me and I banged my head.'

Henrietta was standing to one side and Matthew flashed her a quick glance. 'Who pushed you, Mrs Carradine?' he asked casually, as he felt the woman's scalp with deft fingers that suddenly became still. His face was serious now. 'Just take a look at this, Dr Mason. There's a spongy swelling on the side of the head.'

'Haematoma?' Henrietta suggested, after she'd felt the enlarged area of the scalp

'Could be,' he said, with the gravity still there.

'It was *him*!' Joan cried. 'The one who doesn't like me. He pushed me and I slipped and banged my head on a tree, but there was no blood.'

The two doctors moved away so Mrs Carradine couldn't hear them. 'It sounds as if she's been attacked,' Henrietta said in a low voice, 'but by who?'

'I don't know, but that can wait for the moment,' murmured Matthew. 'If there is a blood clot or something of the sort, it would explain the memory loss, and that could be just the beginning of a series of dangerous issues. We are going to have to call an ambulance. The lady needs to see a neurologist a.s.a.p.'

He turned to the owner of the guest house. 'Could you pack a bag for Mrs Carradine while we phone the hospital, please.'

'Yes, of course,' Lynda replied. 'This is awful. It never dawned on me that she might have been hurt. Who could have done this to her?'

'I don't know,' he said grimly. 'The memory block seems to have cleared a little, but there is still confusion. We need to find out where she goes when she stays here. The people she comes to see will have to know what has happened. Someone must have seen her with them.

'I shall have to notify the police, but in the meantime the most important thing is to get Mrs Carradine into hospital with all speed. The rest of it can wait.'

As they left the guest house after an ambulance had taken Lynda and the injured woman to Accident and Emergency, Henrietta said, 'Maybe there is a reason why she doesn't stay with the people she comes to visit. Perhaps she isn't all that welcome. Or they might not have the room for her to stay with them.'

'It's a mystery,' he said thoughtfully. 'Mrs Carradine could have been imagining it all in her confused state. But there was nothing imaginary about that head wound. If she *was* pushed, it was with a great deal of force for her to have received such damage to the skull.'

'I thought that it was only around the towns and cities that one found such crime,' Henrietta commented, 'but it would appear not.'

He smiled. 'We have our villains in the countryside, too, but maybe not so many of them. The police are going to look into this morning's mystery by calling at Goyt Lodge to examine the injured woman's belongings to see if they give any clue as to why she visits this area so regularly, and will then go to see her at the hospital, which may not be all that easy if she's in Theatre.'

He glanced at her. 'You were comparing the crime rate in town and country a few moments ago. How does health care in the two compare?'

'It's very different from what I'm used to. Everything is at a slower pace and I feel, rightly or wrongly, that because there are fewer patients and more time to deal with them, there's a better standard of care. I dealt with some tough customers in my last job and the workload was tremendous.'

'All I will be asking of you here is a job well done.'

'Yes, I understand that and I *will* do the job properly, but so far I'm not finding you very easy to get to know.'

He pulled the car up by the side of the road and when

he turned towards her there was a glint in the dark eyes looking into hers.

'I'm sorry about that, but as it's only twenty-four hours since we met, don't you think your expectations are a bit high? And if I'm not full of the joys of spring it could be because I've only recently returned from hell on earth, and after what I've seen in that place, there doesn't seem an awful lot to smile about.'

He was right, Henrietta was thinking contritely. Whatever had possessed her to start criticising him? If they'd met under other circumstances she would have had him down as a very presentable member of the opposite sex, in spite of him needing a haircut. Beside Matthew, Miles, the reluctant father, was a non-starter.

This man had lost a wife that he'd loved dearly. He'd not said much about her, but it had come over very strongly in those few moments outside his house, and facing up to a loss that went as deep as that was enough to make anyone sombre.

She didn't know the circumstances of his wife's death as yet, but sensed that the loneliness that he seemed to have surrounded himself with was his way of coping with the pain.

It was wrong, of course. He had all the rest of his life before him and should treasure his wife's memory, but stop brooding and let go. Yet who was she to tell him that? As he'd just pointed out, they'd only known each other a matter of hours.

'I'm sorry,' she told him. 'I asked for that. I've worked for so long in an impersonal atmosphere that I've been overestimating the cosiness of village health care.'

He nodded unsmilingly. 'If it had been the other way round, John staying and myself moving to pastures new, you might have found what you expected. As it is, I'm sorry to disappoint you, Henrietta. If you decide to stay, you're lumbered with me.'

'I'm not planning on going anywhere else,' she told him quickly. 'Even if you sack me, I can't leave the village. I have to stay for the children's sake.'

One of his rare smiles appeared and as it softened the taut lines of his features she knew that whether her stay at the practice turned out to be long or short, it was a face that she wouldn't forget in a hurry.

'So there's your answer,' he said. 'You'll have to put up with me and maybe one day you'll be glad you came, if only to get away from all those tower blocks. So do we have take-off, Dr Mason.'

She smiled back and he noticed that she had dimples. 'Yes, I think so.'

'You only think so?' he enquired dryly. 'You strike me as a woman who knows her own mind.'

'Not always, I'm afraid,' she confessed ruefully

He would have liked to ask her what she'd meant by that. What this pale-skinned woman with the striking hazel eyes, nut-brown hair and dimples had got up to before moving to his patch.

But with a feeling that the atmosphere was in need of lightening, he changed the subject. 'So, apart from this morning's fiasco with the homework, how is the child-minding going?'

'Fine' she said breezily. 'I love children. I'd like a house full of my own one day. But for the time being Mollie and Keiran are the next best thing.'

He smiled 'So you see yourself as an earth mother?'

'No. I was exaggerating. Just two or three will do. And on the subject of children, isn't our next call on a sick child?'

'Yes. The daughter of the local vet, Roger Martin. He rang to ask for a visit as eight-year-old Amy developed a fever during the night. His wife's away so he's coping on his own.'

Henrietta glanced at him sharply. 'No headache? Or rash?'

'Not from the sound of the message we received. I presume you're thinking of meningitis.'

'I was,' she agreed, 'but it doesn't sound like it.'

'Here we are.' He pulled up outside a pretty stone building with a large forecourt and neatly tended flower-beds. 'Let's just hope it's not anything too serious.'

CHAPTER THREE

THE VET lived above his surgery and the moment he opened the door to them Henrietta sensed a lack of cordiality on her companion's part and a degree of discomfort in the attitude of the other man.

'Hello, Matthew, thanks for coming,' he said awkwardly, and pointed to a room across the hallway of the apartment. 'Amy is tucked up in bed all hot and miserable, wanting her mum.'

'Yes, I can imagine,' Matthew said dryly, and Roger Martin looked away. It had been an innocent enough remark, but she sensed that it had been received without warmth.

'I've brought Dr Mason with me,' Matthew went on in the same flat tone. 'She joined the practice yesterday.'

'Why? What's happened to John?' the other man wanted to know.

'Family problems. He's moved down south for a while, so Dr Mason is filling in for him. Shall we take a look at your daughter? What seems to be wrong with her?'

He was perfectly civil. Henrietta couldn't fault his manner, but there was no warmth in it until he perched on the side of

Amy's bed. When they'd appeared she'd turned her face to the wall and her father said, 'Amy has been feverish in the night and very fretful. I've checked for any signs of meningitis and there don't seem to be any, but I'm not prepared to take any chances. That's why I asked for a visit.'

'Tell me where it hurts, Amy,' Matthew said gently.

She rolled over onto her back slowly. A big tear was sliding down her cheek and without speaking she pointed to her throat.

'Does it hurt when you swallow?' he asked in the same gentle tone, and, still without speaking, she nodded.

'Will you open your mouth wide for me and say "Ah",' he asked, and again he received a nod.

The inside of Amy's throat was very inflamed, especially around the tonsils, and when he'd finished examining her, Matthew told the vet, 'Your daughter's got tonsillitis. Has she had it before?'

Roger shook his head. 'No. Or I would have been onto it straight away. She hasn't complained of her throat hurting, but I knew there had to be a reason for the high temperature.'

As Matthew brought out a prescription pad, Roger cleared his throat and with a smile for Henrietta said, 'It's a surprise to hear about John Lomas. I hope you'll be happy in our small community.'

At that moment Matthew's mobile phone rang and he stepped out of earshot to answer it. 'I wasn't expecting Matthew to turn up,' the vet said awkwardly. 'I'm afraid we're not his favourite people. but now I know the situation I'll ask for you on future occasions.'

Henrietta was observing him questioningly and he said, 'It will be easier that way.'

She had no reply to that. Past conflicts didn't interest her, and she didn't want Matthew to find her involved in undercurrents in the practice that were none of her business.

'Give Amy plenty of liquids,' Matthew told Roger when he came back into the room, 'and keep her in bed until she shows some improvement. I'm going to prescribe some low-dosage painkillers suitable for a child, to be given until the inflammation dies down.

'I don't want to prescribe antibiotics at this stage. If it doesn't clear up with the fluids, I'll have to have another think. But let's see how it goes. If it should turn out to be a recurring problem, there may be need for a tonsillectomy, but that would only be suggested if the tonsils were really infected.'

As they drove away from the vet's place Matthew said, 'That was Lynda's husband on the phone from Goyt Lodge.'

'Is there some news of Mrs Carradine?'

'Not regarding her condition. He said they've arrived at A and E and are waiting to see a doctor. It's to be hoped that the removal of the pressure in the skull will bring back her memory if it *is* a haematoma. Then she might be able to give a clearer account of what happened. In the meantime, the mystery of who she comes to visit has been solved. It's her daughter.

'Apparently they meet up each morning in some secluded spot and when she didn't turn up the daughter went to Goyt Lodge to investigate. It seems that Mrs

Carradine and her son-in-law don't get on, and the police think that he found out that she was in the area and attacked her when she went for a stroll in the evening.'

'And what does he have to say?'

'That he never budged out of the house and his wife is backing him up on that, even though her mother is the victim. So it looks as if it is wait-and-see time, until the patient is well enough to be interviewed.'

'I wonder why I was expecting village life to be quiet and peaceful,' Henrietta said in amazement. 'Where are we headed now?'

'To see a young man who is dear to my heart,' said Matthew. 'Daniel Robertson fell off scaffolding on a building site some months ago and fractured his spine. The odds are he will never walk again and there's not much I can do for him, except keep an eye on his pressure points and provide pain relief if he needs it. He's a grand lad. I've never heard him complain, but there must be dark moments when he wonders what the future holds.

'His parents didn't ask for the call. I automatically go to see him every week. Obviously I've missed seeing him while I've been in Pakistan, so want to to make up for it with all speed. You might find it hard to believe, but I always come away from seeing him more humble than when I went in.'

As she watched him chatting with the nineteen-year-old paraplegic, Henrietta was thinking that these two had a special bond. Of courage on the lad's part, and compassion on the doctor's.

When Daniel's mother went into the kitchen to make them a cup of tea, Matthew followed her, and in his absence

Daniel said, 'I owe a lot to Dr Cazalet. He's terrific. He's been there for me all the way ever since I came out of hospital. I've missed him while he's been away.'

Henrietta smiled. 'Yes. I'm sure you must have. I've only just met him, but I can tell already that he's different from all the other doctors I've met.'

'I'm due to go back in hospital in a couple of weeks for some advanced physio,' he said. 'They're going to try to get me more mobile, but I'm not being too optimistic. My legs are paralysed. I have no movement in them because my spinal cord was broken in the fall.'

'That's grim,' she sympathised, and Daniel flashed her a smile.

'It could have been worse. I could have been killed.'

'Yes, you could.' And she thought that when tragedy struck, the attitude of the person or persons involved came from within. It wasn't an age-related thing.

She was silent while walking down the path and settling herself into the passenger seat of the car and Matthew said, 'What are you thinking?'

'That you have many faces.'

He laughed low in his throat. 'Which is preventing you from placing me in any one category? You haven't seen anything yet, Henrietta.'

It was her turn to laugh. 'Now you're trying to scare me.'

'Would I do that.'

'Yes.'

He laughed again and what he had to say next was a surprise. 'I haven't laughed like that in months. You'll have to stick around.'

'I have every intention of doing so, as I don't want to end up on the dole.'

'So that's the only reason you're staying?

'That, and the promise of things to come. You've just told me that I haven't seen anything so far.'

He was stopping the car at the front of the practice and now he was serious. 'Regarding Amy Martin and the tonsillitis, I would never take the reason for my dark moments out on a child. Your presence helped to lighten the embarrassment of Roger and I being in each other's company. Their eldest son was indirectly responsible for my wife's death.'

'Oh, I see,' she breathed.

'I doubt it, but that's the truth of the matter.'

The children had eaten when Henrietta arrived home that evening. On meeting Kate the previous day Henrietta had said she felt that waiting for her to arrive home at any time between six and half past was too late for them to be having their main meal of the day, after being out so early in the morning.

Kate had agreed and suggested that she give them their meal at five, and that food for Henrietta be put to one side to be heated up in the microwave, or kept on a low setting in the oven.

'But what about your meal, Kate?' she'd questioned. 'You're going to be home late each evening since Pamela made these new arrangements with you.'

'I don't mind. As long as the young ones are fed properly,' Kate had assured her, glancing out of the kitchen window to where Mollie and Keiran were playing at the back of the house. 'I shall go down to Matthew's place in the early afternoons and put something in his oven for the two of us. We usually have our evening meal together. So no need to fret, Henrietta.'

And so on this her second day in the practice and the first day of the new arrangements, Henrietta had arrived at The White House to find that the children had been fed and were outside, letting off steam after the day's restrictions.

'Any problems?' she asked Kate, who was ready to leave.

'No,' Kate said with a smile. 'Those two are never any trouble. Their mother rang just as they got in from school and had a chat with them. She said she'd ring you later. Your meal is in the oven.'

Henrietta smiled gratefully. 'Thanks, Kate.'

The older woman nodded and, on the point of leaving, asked, 'How are you getting on with Matthew.'

'I'm not sure what the answer to that is. He's different to any other man I've met, and I sense that he carries a lot of grief around with him.'

Kate nodded sadly. 'Aye, that's for sure. She was a lovely girl, Joanna. Had all her life in front of her, and if the Martin boy had been behaving himself that day she might still be here, but I'm discussing Matthew's business. It's for him to tell you if he wants you to know.'

At that moment the children came chasing into the kitchen, having heard the car pull up, and Kate went on her way, leaving Henrietta even more curious about the man who had become part of her life with what she sensed as some degree of reluctance.

'Henny!' Mollie cried as she flung her arms around her favourite aunt and smothered her with kisses. 'Guess what happened at school today.'

'Er, let me see. You went swimming? Or had a picnic lunch?'

As Mollie shook her head, Keiran giggled, 'She wet her knickers, Aunt Henny.'

'Oh, dear.'

'Not like that!' Mollie cried, red-faced and indignant. 'I fell in a puddle on the playground. Miss found me a dry pair.'

'And where would she have got those from?'

'Someone had left them behind after PE.' Guessing what was coming next, she added, 'They were clean.'

'Good. I'm glad to hear it,' Henrietta said, hiding a smile as she thought of what her sister's reaction would have been. Matthew's comments about Pamela came to mind. It was clear that somewhere along the line she had rubbed him up the wrong way.

When she'd eaten Henrietta put every other thought out of her mind and spent some time with the children, swimming in the pool and playing Snakes and Ladders. Then it was bedtime and as she tucked them up Keiran said out of the blue, 'Mummy says that it's time you got married and had some children, Henny.'

Henrietta raised her eyebrows. 'Does she? Then I'll have to see what I can do, won't I?'

'Have you got a boyfriend?' Mollie wanted to know.

'No. I'm afraid that I haven't.'

'Who would you like to marry?'

'No one at the moment.' Putting an end to their

childish curiosity, she kissed them both goodnight and drew the curtains.

Once downstairs on her own, the day's events came crowding back. The Mrs Carradine mystery, Matthew's lack of cordiality towards the vet and, standing out amongst the other house calls they'd made, Daniel who'd lost the use of his legs.

Then there was the half-tale that Kate had told her about Matthew's wife, and as the day's grand finale, the children's chatter at bedtime. Their innocent questions regarding what *wasn't* happening in her life. She sighed and thought, Out of the mouths of babes.

Tonight she wasn't as in awe of the palatial bedroom as she'd been on her first night in it and she was tired, so sleep soon claimed her. She awoke suddenly to strange noises below her window and as she listened she couldn't believe what she was hearing. Throwing back the bed covers, she padded to the window and gaped at the scene before her.

In the light of a full moon, cows were happily munching away at Pamela and Charles's beautiful front lawn, and hoof marks were appearing right and left in the smooth green turf.

As she stood rigid with dismay two small figures appeared beside her at the window, eyes round as saucers, and she asked of them urgently, 'Children, is there a farm near here.'

They shook their heads and Keiran said, 'Not *so* near, Henny. It's up on the hill behind us.'

'Do you know what the people are called?'

Again there was a shaking of heads.

'Where do Mum and Dad keep the telephone directory?'

There were only two people she knew well enough in the village to ask for help, and there was no way she was going to pass her dilemma on to Kate, so it was going to have to be Matthew. She cringed at the thought but it was what she was going to have to do.

When the phone rang at long past midnight Matthew rolled onto his side and glanced at the clock. When he saw the time he groaned. Night calls weren't passed on to him under existing arrangements. The Doctors' Voluntary Co-operative in the next town dealt with them, so who was it at this hour?

When he picked up the receiver a voice said, 'Matthew, I need your help. You're the only person I know to ask.'

'Is that you, Henrietta?' he asked in surprise.

'Yes,' she told him urgently. 'Can you come over to The White House? I've got a big problem here.'

He was already pulling on his clothes and slipping his feet into his shoes as he asked, 'So what is it that you have to drag me out of bed at this hour? It's not anything to do with the children, is it?'

'No. It's cows. They're on the front lawn and making a mess of it.'

'Cows!' He was laughing. 'Where have they come from.'

'You tell me. You're the country boy.'

'Can't you just shoo them off?'

'No. I can't! I know nothing about cows. They need to go back to where they came from.'

'All right, I'm coming,' he said placatingly. 'I see there's a full moon out there. You don't think they've jumped over it, do you?'

She wasn't amused. 'Every moment you're delaying getting here is adding to the desecration of the front lawn, and I *have* been left in charge of this place, you know.'

'OK, I'm on my way. Don't do anything rash until I get there.'

'I'm not likely to. Just hurry. Please.'

If she wasn't happy about the bovine invasion the children were no such thing. They thought it was exciting and were running from window to window, watching the docile creatures as they munched away.

When Matthew's car pulled up in the drive Henrietta began to calm down. With shouts of encouragement and prods from a stick he'd brought with him, he drove them out on to the lane outside the house within minutes, and then came inside to ring the farm on the hill and ask them to come and pick up their animals.

'They're having a bad time at Gorse Hill farm at the moment,' he told her when he'd made the call. 'Bill Bradley, who owns the place, is in hospital, having a hip replacement, and his son is coping on his own. Paul's only twenty and he lost his mother last year in a road accident. When he arrives I'll go back with him to make sure that everything is all right up there.'

'How do you know the cows belong to that particular farm?' Henrietta asked, with the children wide-eyed beside her.

'I recognise the herd, of course,' he told her, his glance taking in the three of them, Mollie and Keiran flushed and excited in their pyjamas and the new doctor anything but her cool self at that moment in a long silk robe thrown over a matching nightdress.

He knew they weren't her children, but for the uninformed it would be easy to believe they were. The scene before him spoke of families and closeness. He turned away. If Joanna had survived they probably would have had children by now. The drab semi would be filled with laughter and light.

But the last thing he wanted was that this leggy woman who had come into his life should tune into his loneliness. So when he turned back to face her he had himself under control, and as a mud-spattered Land Rover appeared at the bottom of the drive at that moment he was spared further heart-searching.

When Paul saw the lawn he groaned. 'Oh, no, I'm sorry. There's so much to do. I don't know whether I'm coming or going. I must have left the door of the shippon open.'

'I'll come back with you and help get them back where they belong,' Matthew offered.

'I'd be glad of that Dr Cazalet,' Paul said gratefully.

'And I'll get the gardener to sort the lawn out,' Henrietta volunteered. 'So don't upset yourself about that.'

Paul smiled. 'You people are something else.' He turned to the children. 'Why don't you ask your mum to fetch you up to the farm? You can see the animals and I might be able to find you some new-laid eggs for your breakfast.'

Henrietta could tell by their expressions that they thought that this middle-of-the-night excitement was improving by the minute, and there seemed no point in explaining to the young farmer that she wasn't their mother.

'Lock up when we've gone, Henrietta,' Matthew said, adding to the children, 'Back to bed now, kids, or you'll miss the school bus in the morning if you oversleep.'

Henrietta smiled. 'And I will be late for the surgery, and we can't have that.'

It wasn't until Henrietta had the children cuddled one on either side of her in the king-size bed in her room that they went back to sleep, but it wasn't the same for her.

She'd dragged Matthew out of bed in the early hours without so much as a 'would you mind' or 'could you possibly' and now he was on his way to the farm. It wouldn't be surprising if he was thinking that she was more of a liability than an asset.

Sleep did come eventually and she was smiling as she slid into it. She'd coped with down-and-outs, drunkenness, people who lived in penthouses and council house tenants without getting into a flap, but a herd of cows was a different matter.

They didn't oversleep the next morning. The children caught the school bus with time to spare and Henrietta was on time at the practice. The one who was missing was Matthew, and just as she was about to call in her first patient he phoned.

'I'll be with you shortly,' he said. 'I've only just got back from the farm and need to get cleaned up. I stayed on to help with the milking as things up there are a bit chaotic.'

'So you've had no sleep.'

'Er…no. But that's no problem.'

'I'm sorry that I dragged you out of bed.'

'Don't be. If you hadn't done so, I wouldn't have known that the lad needed some help. Did the children get off to sleep all right?'

'Only after they came into my bed. Once they were cuddled up to me they soon nodded off.'

'Good.' He smiled. 'I can't help but feel it is fortunate that your sister wasn't around last night.'

She laughed. 'You could be right. I've already asked the gardener to sort out what needs to be done to restore the lawn back to its former glory, and have told Mollie and Keiran not to mention it when their mummy phones as she might be anxious.'

'And what about the invitation to the farm?'

'They're not likely to forget that. It was the first thing they mentioned when they woke up.'

When Matthew arrived at the surgery a short time later he said, 'I forgot to tell you during our midnight rendezvous that the owner of Goyt Lodge rang me again last night to say that Mrs Carradine's memory is much improved and the unfortunate son-in-law is off the hook. It *was* a haematoma and while she was waiting to go down to Theatre she began to remember what had happened.

'It appears that she was in the habit of going for an evening stroll that took her past what used to be the lodge of the old hall. The people there have two really big dogs, mastiff types that have been trained to keep trespassers at bay. They charge at passersby quite fiercely and it was one of them that jostled the poor lady backwards into the treetrunk.

'Needless to say, the owners will be in trouble for

allowing a dog like that to be off the leash. However, what happened did do some good. Mrs Carradine's son-in-law has been to see her and now they are at least on speaking terms.'

'And there was I thinking that the village was having a mini crime wave, when all the time it was the animals making their presence felt,' Henrietta said. 'Dogs, cows, what next?'

'I'll take you and the children to the farm the first chance I get,' he offered. 'I'm going to be helping with the milking until Bill is back on his feet, so maybe we could combine the two.'

He was letting himself get involved with Henrietta and the children, Matthew thought as he summoned in his first patient of the day. Did he want that? He'd got used to the solitary life and though it wasn't a very happy one, at least it didn't come with any heartbreak.

Daniel Robertson's mother, Joan, was one of those waiting to see him. She'd been on antidepressants ever since her son's accident, and though to everyone else she seemed to be coping admirably, only he knew the depths of her despair at Daniel's condition.

Her husband Mike wasn't much help. He was a caring father, but inclined to only see the surface of things, and was convinced that soon Daniel would be walking again. In fact, the only member of the family to be thinking normally seemed to be Daniel himself, as his mother was sick with apprehension when she thought about the future, and his father in denial.

'So how's it going, Joan?' he asked, as she seated herself on the edge of the chair opposite.

'No different,' she said dispiritedly. 'I've come for a repeat prescription, please.'

'Is the medication helping?'

'Yes, a bit. I'm not so much in a state of dread as I was.'

'Daniel won't want you to be like that, you know,' Matthew said gently. 'He is an amazing young man who could set us all an example. When I called the other day he said he intended getting involved in paraplegic sporting activities, and I can't think of anything better to keep him fit and happy.'

'Not even being able to walk?'

'Of course not. That would be the answer to everything. Joan, life isn't like that. Sometimes we have to take what is on offer and do the best we can with it.' He squeezed her hand and smiled. 'If I had a son I would want him to be like that lad of yours, brave and clear thinking. Go home and count your blessings. At least you've still got him. He could have been killed in that fall.'

Joan managed a watery smile. 'Yes, he could have. You're right, of course. Thanks, Matthew, for taking the time to hear my woes.'

'That's what I'm here for,' he told her, and imagined that her step was lighter going out than coming in.

When she'd gone he sat staring into space. 'If I'd had a son,' he'd said. and thought if that young idiot, the Martin boy, hadn't been clowning about on the edge of one of the biggest drops in the area he might have had one, or a daughter like young Mollie up at The White House.

But the fact remained that he hadn't. Joanna had been taken from him in the cruellest way and life had to go on, and a big part of it was centred around his patients, anxious to tell him about their aches and pains. As he called the next one in he had a smile for them.

When Henrietta arrived home that evening Kate said, 'The children have been telling me about the cows last night. Good job their mother wasn't around. She'd have thrown a fit. You sent for Matthew, I believe.'

'Yes. I was panicking. He was brilliant. Had them off the lawn quickly, but I felt dreadful afterwards, as he got involved with helping out at the farm. When I saw him this morning he hadn't been to bed.'

'I shouldn't worry about it. He'll soon let you know if he's got any complaints. There's no beating about the bush with that nephew of mine. I wish sometimes that he would soften up a bit.'

That would make two of us, Henrietta thought, but she'd had no fault to find with him last night. It was a shame that he didn't want to move on and find himself a new wife who would give him children. She'd seen the way he looked at Mollie and Keiran. But if Matthew was determined to spend his days between the surgery and his house, with little or no social life, he wasn't going to meet anybody that way.

She was resigned to her own social life being pretty restricted during the coming months, with the job, the house and, even more important, the children to care for. But in her case it would be from circumstance rather than choice.

Matthew rang late in the evening and when she heard his voice her spirits lifted. 'I've just had a call from Jackie Marsland's husband,' he said. 'She's hanging in there with the baby. They've told her that she has to have complete bed rest until the bleeding stops, and will have to take it easy all the time during the pregnancy, which is catastrophic for the café.

'But her husband's family are rallying round now they know the score, and they'll manage somehow or other. I'm sorry to break into your evening, Henrietta, but as she was the first of our patients that you were involved with, I thought you'd like to know.'

'You're right,' she told him, touched by his thoughtfulness. 'I've been wondering how things were going for her. I have a feeling that she might still miscarry, but do hope I'm wrong.'

'You're not alone in that. I think the same, but the hospital seems optimistic, so we'll have to see how it goes. Are the children asleep?'

'Yes.'

'And what are *you* doing?'

'Adjusting.'

'What do you mean?'

'Adjusting to country life, cows and all. I love it, Matthew, but then I always knew I would.'

She didn't tell him that finding a man like him as part of the package was going to make village living even more pleasant.

CHAPTER FOUR

IN THE week after the episode with the cows, Matthew said one morning, 'Paul Bradley at the farm has reminded me that the children have been invited to see the animals.'

'So he meant what he said?' asked Henrietta.

'Yes, and so did I. I'll take the three of you up there. How about Saturday afternoon before I get involved with the evening milking?'

'Are you sure that you want to do that?' she asked, picking up on something in his tone.

Matthew hesitated. If he told her the truth, it would be that he wasn't. Not because he didn't want to be with her and the children—far from it. But because for the first time since losing Joanne he was dropping his guard. Letting the new doctor at the practice and her two enchanting charges make him feel human again, which was all very nice, but supposing it didn't last. That the moment her sister came back for her children Henrietta would be gone. The novelty of living in the countryside might have worn off by the time Pamela and her husband came back.

But he wasn't going to admit he was having those sorts of

thoughts to Henrietta. She could easily think that he was presuming too much, so he told her, 'Yes, of course I'm sure.'

'You've been spending a lot of time at the farm, haven't you?' she said wryly. 'And it's all my fault.'

He smiled. 'Why? Because you sent for me in your hour of need? I would have been upset if I hadn't known about the lad struggling on his own up there. You did us both a favour.'

'I don't understand why they haven't hired some extra help while his father's been in hospital,' she said. 'It would seem the obvious thing to do.'

'They might have done if they could have afforded it. Most of the farmers just about make ends meet, and for these two guys there's no home baked bread coming out of the oven and nourishing casseroles after a hard day's work.

'With the woman of the house gone, it's a case of living out of tins and sending for take-aways, which is not the cheapest way of eating. It's probably what I'd be doing if Kate wasn't around. So, shall we say four o'clock on Saturday?'

'Yes, that will be fine,' she told him.

The routine at the practice was that the doctors took it in turn to do the short Saturday morning surgery and this week it was Matthew's turn.

'I'll do the surgery if you like,' Henrietta offered. 'It will give you a free morning if you're going to be taking us to the farm in the afternoon.'

'What will you do with the children?'

'Take them with me. It's only for a couple of hours and they won't get in the way.'

'No need to do that. You can drop them off at my place. I'll look after them. If you are going to fill in for me, I'm going to spend the morning attacking the jungle that is my garden. They can help me if they like.'

'They'll love that.' She smiled. 'Especially if they find any worms.'

He was doing it again, Matthew thought afterwards. Letting his barriers down. Maybe it was because the memory was so clear of her standing there in the silk nightwear with the children on either side of her on the night that the cows had come. It went with the expensive perfume that he'd commented on when she'd first started at the practice.

Henrietta hadn't known it was the same as Joanna used to wear and he'd been less than civil about it, instead of telling her what was in his mind. What had he been expecting her to wear, he wondered, winceyette at night and lucky bag scent during the day?

When Henrietta went to pick up Mollie and Keiran after the surgery was over, she found the three of them having a cold drink beside a parched looking lawn, and when Matthew suggested she join them she shook her head.

'No, thanks just the same,' she told him. 'But if you'd like have lunch with us, you'll be very welcome. It would be my way of saying thanks for looking after the children.'

'I enjoyed it.' He shrugged, and wished she'd been there to make up the foursome. 'And I'm the one who should be saying thanks to you for taking the surgery for me. Was it busy?'

'No, not really, but I did have a couple of patients who wouldn't have wanted to wait until Monday to see one of us.'

'Such as?'

'Does the name Craig Carter ring a bell?'

'Yes. He has the ladies' hairdressers at the other end of the village. What was wrong with Craig?'

'Two badly swollen hands. I think the inflammation is allergy related. He's been using some kind of new perming solution. Said he wears gloves when he's applying it, but I don't see how he can have been.'

'So you told him to lay off it, did you?'

'Yes, and prescribed an antihistamine to take the soreness away. Even so, I can't see him doing any hairdressing for a few days.'

'And who was the other?'

'A mother with a young baby that has nappy rash,' said Henrietta. 'She uses the terry towelling squares, a rare practice now. When I asked what kind of washing powder she used, I found the reason for baby's sore bottom. She left with a prescription for a water repellent, emollient cream and the suggestion that she change to soap flakes, or one of the other gentler washing products.

'Both patients should have been in plenty of time to catch the chemist before they shut at midday. And now, getting back to ourselves, are you going to join us for lunch?'

After a morning spent with the children Matthew was looking more relaxed than she'd ever seen him, and she thought this was what he was short of. A chance to unwind in a family setting instead of shutting himself away in that ghastly looking house. If his wife had been as lovely as

Kate had described her, she wouldn't want him to be carrying the burden of grief for the rest of his life.

'I'd love to,' he said, and watched the dimples appear as she flashed him a smile.

'Good. Shall we say one o'clock?'

'Sure,' he said easily.

It was clear that the children had no objections to the arrangement. They were nodding in enthusiastic agreement, and Keiran said, 'We're going to have lunch on the patio, aren't we, Henny? Bacon butties and gingerbread men that Mrs Crosby has made for us.'

'Oh, well, if Mrs Crosby made the gingerbread men, I'll have to come, won't I?' he told them. 'She used to make them for me when I was little.'

'Did she?' Keiran was suitably impressed.

Matthew grinned. 'Mmm, she did.'

When they arrived home Henrietta said, 'Right, children. First of all your hands need a good washing after helping Dr Cazalet in the garden. Then you can put a nice cloth on the table out on the patio and lay out some cutlery and plates. While you're doing that I'm going upstairs to change out of my working clothes, and when I come down we'll see what's in the fridge.'

She'd invited Matthew to have lunch with them on the spur of the moment and now wasn't sure if she'd done the right thing. Maybe it would be more sensible if they didn't get involved in each other's lives, but so far he'd been the one making all the moves and she didn't want him to feel it was all one-sided.

He arrived at just before one o'clock and when she opened the door to him with a plastic apron over the jeans and cotton shirt that she'd changed into, there was something in his glance that made her colour rise.

'You are so different from your sister it just isn't true,' he said in a low voice. 'The children are so lucky to have you.'

Not knowing what to say, Henrietta babbled, 'Do you know what they said to me the other night when I was tucking them up in bed?'

'Er…no. But, then, I'm not likely to, am I.'

'They said that their mother thinks it is time I had some children of my own.'

'And what did you say to that?'

'What could I say? I told them I would see what I could do, but that wasn't enough. They wanted to know if I'd got a boyfriend, and when I said no, they asked who I wanted to marry. The answer to that was no one, and I beat a speedy retreat.'

She smiled, but Matthew didn't and she thought with a sinking feeling that the description of her non-existent social life might have sounded like a come-on to a man in his position, but she needn't have worried.

'There's a lot to be said for the single life,' he said coolly, and moved smoothly on to another topic. 'The children need to call me something less formal than Dr Cazalet. What do you suggest?'

'Matthew, I suppose, if you don't mind that. Though it is rather going to the other extreme.'

'I don't mind at all.'

Henrietta was grateful that Mollie and Keiran kept the

conversation going while they had lunch. She was still feeling uncomfortable about the way she'd babbled on about their interest in her love life.

Matthew's thoughts were running in a different direction and she would have been surprised to know that he was telling himself that she wouldn't be unattached for long.

He'd seen one or two of the local romeos eyeing up the new doctor.

Why couldn't John have taken on someone—anyone— else? he thought grimly. Then he wouldn't be acting against his better judgement by using the children as an excuse to get to know Henrietta away from the surgery. They were delightful, but it was her that he couldn't get out of his mind.

The life he'd been living since losing Joanna had been a safe sort of existence. No one to be taken from him. No one to ache over or worry about, except Kate, who he loved dearly.

When they'd finished eating he got up to go and when the children protested he told them, 'I'll be back to take you to the farm in a couple of hours.' He turned to Henrietta. 'Thanks for the lunch. My place really will look drab after dining here. Maybe today is what I've been needing to give me an incentive to do some refurbishing.'

'Make sure you choose sunshine colours if you do,' she said. 'Pale gold, cream, honey…'

'I'll remember that,' he told her unconvincingly. 'Maybe I should ask you to be my interior designer if I ever get around to it.'

She smiled. 'You have only to ask. I could bring light into your life with a few tins of paint and a pasteboard.'

He didn't take her up on that, just waved to the children and said, 'I'll see you later.'

As he drove home Matthew was thinking that she didn't know it, but Henrietta had already brought some light into his life, and something else that she couldn't be expected to know was that he wasn't sure whether he was glad or sorry.

As the children eyed the tiny, flat-nosed piglets snuffling around their mother in the pen where they were kept, and dodged some nosy geese waddling towards them, Matthew was smiling.

'Don't tell me that they live in the country and have never been to a farm,' he said in amused disbelief.

'Oh, I'm sure they will have,' she told him. 'I've heard Charles say that he goes to one of the farms for free-range eggs. It might be this one, for all we know. They're just enjoying everything going on around them. The noises from the milking shed will be adding to the thrill of the place as they'll recognise them from the night the dairy herd came to visit us.'

Bill Bradley was home from hospital but not yet fit for work. The two doctors knew it would be some time before he could take up where he'd left off in the running of the place. But Paul was already looking less harassed now his father was home, and as the older man watched the children from the farmhouse window there was a smile on his face.

'It's good to see your dad back with you,' Matthew told Paul. 'I'll go and have a word with him while Mollie and Keiran get to know your animals.'

'Dr Cazalet can do anything,' Paul said when he'd gone inside. 'Having him around has stopped me from going crackers. He even baked me a cake when he was here the other day and stuck a stew in the oven, and they were just as good as my mum used to make.'

'Yes. I can believe it,' she told him.

She already knew that Matthew was a man of many faces and it would seem that he was also a man of many talents. She supposed that Kate wasn't always around to make him a meal and he wasn't the type to starve. It was a pity that among his accomplishments he wasn't able to turn his private life around.

When Matthew came out of the farmhouse he said, 'I've given Bill a prescription for painkillers. He has a limited supply from the hospital that should cover the next couple of days, but may need more until the soreness wears off. I'll still be coming up each day to help with the milking so I'll be able to keep my eye on him.' He looked around him. 'Where are the children?'

'In the shed with Paul. Renewing their acquaintance with the cows.'

He smiled. 'Right. So when they come out I'll run you back to The White House and then come back for the milking.'

'What time will you be done here?'

'Why?'

'You've given up most of your day already.'

'I should be home about sixish and then the evening will be mine. You've no need to worry.'

'Will Kate have made you a meal?'

'No. She goes to the town with her friends on Saturdays, but I do know how to open a tin of baked beans.'

'And you also know how to bake a cake and…'

'Cobble a casserole together? You have been talking to Paul, haven't you. As a matter of fact, I always dine at the Goose on Saturday evenings. I have a regular booking.'

'Where's that?'

'The hotel down a leafy lane off the road that leads out of the village. So, you see, I'm not going to die from malnutrition. But thanks for the thought, Henrietta. If you hadn't been childminding you could perhaps have joined me.'

Not quite sure if she'd heard him correctly, she made no comment and instead said, 'And do you make a night of it?'

He shook his head and she thought, Surely he doesn't go home to that empty house the moment he's finished eating? But he was about to surprise her further.

'No. Once I've eaten I go and get a few beers and go round to Daniel's house to play cards or watch television with him. It gives his parents the chance to have a night out together, and I know that Joan wouldn't want to leave him with anyone else. And I enjoy it. He's a great kid.'

When he'd taken them home and gone back to the farm, Henrietta couldn't stop thinking about him. Matthew was something else. What other man would spend Saturday evening with a patient to give the young man's parents some time off? Or get up at crack of dawn to help with the milking at a nearby farm and then do a full day's work at the practice, before going back to the farm again to assist with the second milking of the day? When she saw him again on Monday she was going to ask him how he'd found time to bake a cake.

It had been a lovely day. Mollie and Keiran had enjoyed every minute of it and so had she. She wasn't sure whether Matthew had or not. He wasn't one to show his feelings, but he had accepted her invitation to lunch, which was a step in the right direction, if only she knew what the right direction was.

When Henrietta asked him about the cake and the casserole on Monday morning he laughed and said, 'I suppose I'd better come clean. Kate had prepared the casserole. All I had to do was put it in the oven. But I did make the cake. It was a Victoria sponge, which, as you probably know, doesn't take long. And while it was in the oven I helped with the milking.'

'And I suppose that afterwards you filled it with whipped cream and raspberry jam,' she teased.

'No way. The raspberry jam, yes, but no whipped cream. I was dying of hunger myself by that time.'

'Amazing.'

'What do you mean?'

'The fact that you just knocked together a Victoria sponge, and I suppose it rose beautifully.'

He was smiling and she thought how it transformed the strong lines of his face. He ought to do it more often.

'As a matter of fact, it did,' he said as he seated himself behind his desk and made ready to greet his first patient of the day. As Henrietta went to her own room to do likewise she was thinking that the settling in period at the practice was proving much easier than she'd thought it would be. She was going to be happy there. A rapport was forming between herself and the man she'd been so unsure of at their first meeting, and it felt good.

'Who's the girl with the long hair and long legs?' Gary Fenton asked as he seated himself opposite Matthew in the middle of the morning.

'That's Dr Henrietta Mason, who is sharing the running of the practice with me,' he said, glowering at Gary, the owner of the local garage. 'And I don't think she'd be too keen on your description of her.'

Gary was in his late forties and known to like women, especially other men's wives, and Matthew was surprised how irritated he felt at what the man had said.

It was the way the garage owner talked about every young woman he met and under other circumstances he wouldn't have taken much notice, but Henrietta was different.

'I'd would be careful what you say if you have to consult Dr Mason over anything, Gary. You might end up with an enema, or at the least castor oil.'

Unabashed, Gary said, 'It's funny you should say that, Doc. It's my colon I've come about.'

Trying to keep a straight face, Matthew asked, 'So what's the problem?'

'I'm losing blood.'

'Right, so take your pants off and I'll examine you.'

When he'd finished the examination Matthew said, 'I can't see or feel anything suspicious, but I can tell you what you have got. You've got haemorrhoids and that is likely to be where the blood is coming from. I'm going to give you some ointment to spread on the affected area and stick to a healthy diet. Cut out the stodgy foods and eat plenty of fruit and veg.'

When he'd gone Matthew knew that his annoyance with Gary was because Saturday was still fresh in his memory. Working in the garden with those two great kids. Then Henrietta appearing after the morning surgery and inviting him to lunch. Later in the afternoon there had been their visit to the farm and the pleasure of watching Mollie and Keiran with the animals. He hadn't felt so happy and relaxed in years.

Was this what he'd been waiting for? he wondered. Kate had told him often enough that he needed to get on with his life. That it was no fault of his that Joanne had died, and she wouldn't want him to be grieving for evermore, but it never brought any comfort.

He and Joanna had known each other since they'd been children and when he'd come back to the village after getting a degree in medicine they'd met up again and fallen madly in love.

She'd been a teacher at the village school and had loved it. They'd often talked about the children they would have one day.

When the morning surgery was over and they stopped for a quick bite Henrietta said, 'I like wallpapering and painting. If you want to brighten up your house I would love to help. I'd have to bring the children with me, of course, and it would have to be at the weekend, but what do you think?'

In view of their ripening acquaintance she was expecting him to say yes but, unaware of the sombre road his thoughts had been travelling along, she was being too optimistic.

Without showing any interest in the suggestion, he said, 'Perhaps some time, yes. But I don't feel there's any rush. It's good of you to offer, but I'm not out to compete with your sister's residence.'

'I'm sorry,' she said hurriedly. 'I didn't mean to be intrusive. I just thought you might look forward to going home more at the end of each day if the house was bright and cheerful.'

He was being boorish and ungrateful, he thought. Making matters worse, he said, 'Maybe I don't want that, Henrietta. Have you ever thought of that?'

'Oh! For goodness' sake!' she exploded. 'Stop wallowing in self-pity, Matthew! I wish I'd never mentioned the decorating. You can rest assured it won't happen again.'

Leaving him to digest that, she went across the road to the baker's to buy something for her lunch, and wondered why the man working on the garage forecourt kept staring at her.

Why couldn't he have accepted Henrietta's offer in the spirit it had been meant? Matthew thought dismally when she'd gone. He knew there had been nothing behind it except a genuine desire to brighten up his house, and he'd thrown it back in her face just as they had been getting to know and like each other. He was crazy.

During the afternoon he rang Kate at The White House and told her that he was going to one of the DIY outlets on the edge of the town and would be late home for his meal.

'No problem,' she said. 'I'll do something that I don't need to cook until you arrive.'

Matthew made his purchases, bearing in mind what Henrietta had said about sunshine colours, and dropped the large cans of paint and rolls of wallpaper off at the surgery in the hope that when she saw them the next morning no explanations would be necessary.

It was a vain hope. He'd put the materials he'd bought in the passage outside their two consulting rooms, so that she couldn't miss seeing them, but there was no comment forthcoming. In the end he went into her room and said, 'All right, Henrietta. What you see out there is my way of saying sorry. I would be grateful for your help and your forgiveness for my churlishness yesterday.

'My reluctance to take you up on your offer was nothing personal. It's just that I feel that those who walk alone are less likely to come unstuck. But when I thought about it afterwards I knew you were right. My house is crying out for a lick of paint so, yes, please, I would welcome your help. Especially as it will mean seeing Mollie and Keiran again. I've even bought two small paintbrushes for them.'

She was smiling. 'They'll love that, Matthew, and so will I. And when we've finished the decorating, maybe new carpets and curtains, do you think?'

He returned her smile. 'Why not? But let's get the decorating sorted first.'

She was serious now. 'I have an apology to make, too. I shouldn't have said what I did about self-pity. I haven't known you long and it was extremely presumptuous of me to be making such judgements. I do hope you'll forgive me.'

He sighed. 'There's nothing to forgive. You're the first person who has ever come out and said what everyone else is probably thinking. If you'd known me any longer, you might have accepted that the way I am is me, when it isn't at all. I wasn't always like this.'

'Have you ever treated yourself for depression?' she asked carefully.

'No. I couldn't be bothered. I've treated plenty of other people, though. But enough of that. Do we start the revamp this weekend, or have you other things to do?'

'No. I haven't. This weekend will be fine. Will you be able to find some surfaces for Mollie and Keiran to paint?'

'Sure thing, and I'll be responsible for lunch.'

Laughter was glinting in her eyes. 'Are you going to make a Victoria sponge?'

'I doubt it. It might not be as successful a second time and I wouldn't want to lose face,' he told her jokingly. 'How about crisps, sandwiches and chocolate biscuits, with suitable drinks?'

'Sounds fine. They'll love that, and they'll love seeing you again. Can I come round to view the property before Saturday, so it's clear in my mind what we will be attempting?'

'Yes, if you like. But be prepared. That place of mine is clean but claustrophobic and crying out for some tender loving care. You'll find it very different from your present accommodation.'

'Possibly I will, but there's such a thing as a place being too grand. I feel a bit lost in my sister's house. Something between that and my poky flat would suit me fine. When it gets nearer the time for Pamela and Charles to come back, I'm going to start looking around the village for *my* dream home.'

'So you're intending staying after they come back for the children? You aren't going back to urban life?'

She was gazing through a nearby window at the peaks rising in the distance and the stone cottages and quaint shops across the way.

'Not after having a taste of village life. Even if you don't need me any more when John comes back. I'll find some way of earning a living so that I can stay here.'

'And why do you think I wouldn't want you to be part of the practice permanently?' he asked. 'As you said earlier, we haven't known each other long, but I've got your measure, just as unfortunately you seem to have got mine, and I have no complaints. I enjoy working with you.'

'Even though I'm not prepared to let you vegetate?'

'It might be because of that.' He turned to go back into his own room. 'How about I take you round to my place tomorrow in the lunch-hour?'

She nodded. 'Yes, that will be fine.'

'And in the meantime I'd like you to come with me to visit one of our patients who is a delightful elderly lady and is always on at me to employ a lady doctor in the practice.'

'She soon gets embarrassed, does she?'

'No, nothing like that. It's equality of the sexes that she's concerned about.'

'Right. I don't see anything wrong in that.'

'I didn't think you would,' he said dryly. 'Margot

Chilton is an artist. If you stop by the window of the gallery next to the post office you will always see some of her paintings on display, and they are quite something.

'She's become very arthritic of late and lives in constant dread of her hands becoming too stiff to paint. Her mobility is already affected and that is why I visit her, instead of Margot having to come to the surgery.

'Today we aren't going on a consultation. I'm taking you there so I can introduce you to her so she can see that at last we have a woman doctor in the practice.'

Henrietta smiled across at Matthew from the passenger seat of his car. 'So you aren't going to tell her that you had nothing to do with my appointment and that on first acquaintance you weren't impressed?'

'Absolutely not!' he said in mock horror. 'It might affect my standing with Margot. I would only do that if she didn't approve of you, and from where I'm sitting that's not likely to happen.'

'You're something else!' she told him with a twinkle.

He had no comment to make about that. Instead he said, 'I've been wondering why I've started to feel different and have come to the conclusion it's from all the laughing I've been doing lately. My face just isn't used to it and you are to blame for that, Henny.'

'Am I really? Well, that's good news,' she said softly. 'You are getting better, Dr Cazalet. I can't guarantee a cure, but some improvement is always welcomed by we GPs.'

They stopped in front of a small detached house with mullioned windows and a garden that was a riot of colour.

When Matthew took her round to the back a voice hailed them from out of a gazebo in the centre of the garden.

As they approached Henrietta saw that its occupant was a small but sturdy-looking woman with snow-white hair above an apple-cheeked face that was displaying a broad smile of welcome.

'Matthew!' she cried delightedly. 'You're back. And who is this you have with you?' Before he could answer she said, 'Let me guess. You've found yourself a new love at last, and you've brought her to meet me.'

Their reactions were completely opposite. A bright red Henrietta was wishing the ground beneath her feet would open up and swallow her, while an expressionless Matthew said smoothly, 'You've got it wrong. Margot. That's one of the things you're always urging me to do, but there is also another. Have you forgotten?'

Margot was observing him blankly and he went on. 'A lady doctor, yes? This is Dr Henrietta Mason who has joined the practice. I've brought her to meet you.'

'Oh, dear!' Margot said apologetically. 'I have put my foot in it, haven't I, Dr Mason? Do forgive me both of you.' She got slowly to her feet and shook Henrietta's hand with returning confidence. 'You must both come inside for a coffee and you can tell me all about yourself, my dear.'

'Are you resident in the village?' the elderly woman asked when they were seated in a sitting room full of mahogany furniture and chintz drapes.

'Er…yes, for the moment,' Henrietta told her. 'I'm looking after my sister's children for a few months while she and her husband are away.'

'And who would that be? I know most of the residents.'

'Pamela Wainright from The White House.'

'Ah! Yes. I know the Wainrights. They have two lovely children. Pamela and Charles always invite me when they are having a dinner party.'

She turned to Matthew, who hadn't spoken since they'd gone into the house, and asked, 'How was Pakistan, my dear?'

'Rewarding in a remote sort of way, but not pleasant, Margot.'

'I prayed for you to come home safely,' she said, and Henrietta thought if she herself had known him then, she would have done the same.

'And it must have worked, as here I am,' he said, forcing a smile.

When they were ready to leave Margot clasped Henrietta's hand and said, 'I shall look forward to getting to know you, my dear, and you will forgive my awful *faux pas*, I hope.'

'Yes, of course,' Henrietta told her, avoiding the glance of the man beside her.

CHAPTER FIVE

'I AM SO sorry about that,' he said through clenched teeth as they drove off into the summer afternoon. 'The last thing I'd anticipated was Margot jumping to such crazy conclusions and causing you embarrassment.

'There's been a conspiracy going on for some time amongst those who know me to get me married off again. Your sister once invited me to one of her dinner parties with the idea of parading me as an eligible widower, and when I realised I was not pleased, especially as it wasn't all that long after I'd lost Joanna.'

'So *that's* what you've got against Pamela,' Henrietta breathed. 'She can be a bit insensitive at times. But Margot meant no harm and I won't lose any sleep over it, so don't be upset.'

She had to feel sorry for him. Surely the people who cared about him should respect his feelings regarding his dead wife and let Matthew decide if and when he was going to marry again.

'So you're not offended.'

'Of course I'm not,' she said quietly. 'How could I be? None of it was of your doing. Why don't we just forget it?'

'If you say so,' he agreed wryly, and then added, as if reluctant to let the matter drop, 'You'll be thinking that being around me is not a happy place to be.'

'And why should I think that?'

'Yesterday I threw your offer of help in your face. Today Margot is trying to marry you off to me.'

'I can think of worse things than that,' she told him laughingly.

'Such as?'

'A herd of cows on my sister's immaculate lawn.'

He was smiling now and she began to relax until he said, 'I'll have to bear that in mind. You feel that being married to me would be a lesser fate than dairy cows under your window. I hope there might be a vote of confidence somewhere in that comment, but I'm not too sure. Are you like that with all animals?'

'No, of course not,' she protested quickly, wondering whatever had made her joke about being married to him. 'I like dogs, cats and horses, but cows are an unknown quantity.'

By the time they got back to the surgery the waiting room was filling up again and as they were about to go to their separate rooms Matthew said, 'Don't forget to tell the children about Saturday. Do they have any old clothes to wear?'

'There will be some somewhere,' she told him, and felt a rush of pleasure at the thought of what they had planned for the coming Saturday. Mollie and Keiran would love it when they knew they would be painting with real paint.

How was she going to cope when Pamela and Charles

came for them? Life would be really empty then. She supposed Pamela was right. It was time she thought about having a family of her own.

But first she had to find herself a husband, and after the disastrous end to her affair with Miles and the hurt it had left behind, she wasn't feeling too confident on that score.

But after his departure from her life another man had stepped into it. .Matthew had caught her imagination from the start. Like her, he was wary of being hurt again, though his pain covered a much wider spectrum. Yet she sensed that there was warm blood in his veins. There was nothing shallow about Matthew Cazalet. He was a man of deep feelings and, she imagined, deep desires.

Douglas Hoyle was the practice manager. A retired accountant, he did the job on a part-time basis, and dealt with most of it at home, but occasionally he asked for a meeting between the two doctors and himself. At the end of the day Matthew said, 'Douglas wants a meeting. He's suggested tomorrow after the late surgery, but I've told him that you have family commitments and also it would mean Kate having to stay late at your place. Have you any thoughts on the matter?'

'Not unless you both came to The White House in the evening.'

'You wouldn't mind?'

'No. Not as long as the children were in bed. I don't like them to be up late during the week as they have to catch the school bus at such an early hour. Do you think that would be a suitable arrangement for Douglas?'

'I don't see why not.'

'And you?'

'Yes, of course. After I've been to help with the milking. This should be my last week. Bill says he's ready to get back in harness for some of the lighter jobs. So is tomorrow evening all right?'

Henrietta nodded. 'Yes. Once the children are in bed I either read, or spend some time going over the day's happenings with regard to my patients.'

She wasn't going to tell him that he figured largely in her thoughts, too. His dismay at being linked with her in a romantic sort of way earlier that afternoon was something she wasn't going to forget in a hurry, even though she'd treated it light-heartedly.

'Some of the consultations are done and forgotten, while others stay so clearly in the mind that I bring the memory home with me and can't always put it to rest,' she continued.

Matthew frowned. 'Such as?'

'Late this afternoon I had a patient with what could turn out to be a brain tumour. All the symptoms were there—headaches, periodical loss of vision, muscle weakness, to name a few. I've referred him to the neurology and oncology departments at the hospital for an urgent appointment and can't get him out of my mind. He's in his twenties and hasn't been married long. They're expecting their first baby and this has been thrown at them.'

'What's his name?'

'He's one of your patients. David Lorimer. You were

fully booked for the next few days and he didn't want to wait. He was feeling so ill and traumatised by all the things happening to him that he agreed to see me.'

'No!' Matthew groaned. 'Not Dave Lorimer! He's a great lad. His father is in charge of the village brass band. Dave plays the drums and Sue, his wife, the cornet. Did he say how long he'd had the symptoms?'

'They've have come on pretty suddenly, and I think he should be seeing you over something as serious as this, Matthew. You know him so much better than I do and he'll draw comfort from that.'

He nodded. 'I'll pop round to see his dad tonight. He lives quite near me. Maybe he can put me in the picture before I talk to Dave.'

'Supposing he hasn't told his father?'

'That is a possibility, of course, and I shall be wary of what I say when I get there. I can always tell Alan I'm thinking of joining the band again.'

'You were in it?' asked Henrietta in surprise.

Matthew shrugged. 'Yes, once.'

'And are you going to join again?'

'No. Not really.'

'Why not?'

'I'm out of practice, for one thing. I haven't played since before…' His voice trailed away. 'You know what I was going to say, don't you?'

'Yes. I do,' she told him gravely. 'So what instrument did you play?'

'Trombone. We have a band concert in the village every year. It took place this time while I was in Pakistan, and you hadn't yet come to work and live here. For anyone into brass bands, it's quite an event.'

'So why don't you join again? There's something about a man in a uniform,' she teased. 'What colours do they wear?'

He smiled 'Red and black. They rehearse on Thursday nights in the Scout hut.'

When Henrietta arrived home that evening and Kate heard her telling Mollie and Keiran what was planned for Saturday, she couldn't believe it. 'You've actually persuaded Matthew to do some decorating?' she said. 'That's wonderful! You must have the magic touch, Henrietta. I've tried countless times and he didn't want to know.'

'He didn't agree at first when I asked him,' she explained, 'but he must have had a rethink and went to buy the materials last night.'

'So that's what he went to the DIY place for.'

'Yes, it must have been,' she agreed, and turned to Mollie and Keiran, 'So what do you think of that, kids? We're going to make Dr Cazalet's house really posh.'

'We think it's great,' they chorused, and, with Henrietta following behind, they rushed upstairs to find some old clothes for painting in.

When Henrietta saw the inside of Matthew's house the next day she wanted to weep. Not because it was as bad as he'd described it. It was far from that, and the decorating, new carpets and curtains would transform it into a pleasant home.

It was the overwhelming feeling of emptiness in the

rooms that was upsetting her, though she supposed it was to be expected if he just used it as somewhere to eat and sleep.

She'd looked each room over in turn and in the main bedroom averted her eyes from the king-size bed where he spent his lonely nights. There was a big photograph of a merry-eyed woman with short golden hair and a smiley mouth on the dressing-table and she didn't know whether to comment, or pretend she hadn't seen it.

Matthew was watching her. She could feel the intensity of his gaze and when she looked up and their eyes met, she knew that he was waiting to see what she had to say.

'She was beautiful, your Joanna,' she'd said softly. 'Really lovely. You must have been very happy.'

'Yes. We were,' was all he said. 'So what do you think of the house?'

'It's nowhere near as horrible as you made out,' she told him. 'But the whole place is badly in need of a facelift, and it will take us some weeks to put it right.'

'And you are still prepared to get involved?'

'Yes, I am, because it won't get done if I'm not. You'll shelve it again.'

'No, I won't, Henrietta. Remember I've bought the paint and paper, and now have just one question.' He was smiling. 'Who's going to be the gaffer and who's going to be the labourer?'

'I can't believe you feel the need to ask,' she told him in mock surprise. 'I'm in charge, of course.'

When Matthew and Douglas arrived at eight o'clock in the summer evening Henrietta opened the door to them dressed in a peach cotton sundress and strappy sandals. Matthew had only ever seen her with her hair down, but tonight it was piled on the top of her head in shining coils held in place with a gold comb, and the effect was such that he found himself taking a deep breath as hazel eyes, clear and untroubled, met his.

She stepped back to let them in and he caught a whiff of the perfume that he'd asked her not to wear at the surgery. Was it her way of telling him that he might rule the roost during the day, but her free time was a different matter?

When she'd worn it before he'd made a big issue of it and regretted it. He had no intention of going down that road once more, but felt that he owed her an explanation. Not in front of Douglas, though.

The elderly practice manager was looking around him, suitably impressed, and as Henrietta showed them into the sitting room he said, 'By Jove. Henrietta, this place is amazing!'

She smiled. 'It isn't mine, you know, Douglas. I'm childminding and house-minding at the same time.'

'Have you had time to eat?' she asked Matthew as she brought in a tray of drinks and some nibbles.

'Yes. I did the milking in record time then went home and showered before eating the meal that Kate had made for us. And now here I am, ready to hear what Douglas has to tell us.'

In truth, he was not in the mood for facts and figures at all. He was wishing that he could spend the evening with just Henrietta, chatting, strolling around the grounds and peeping in on the children. Hopefully Douglas would go early once they'd concluded their business and then he would have her to himself.

When they were all seated the elderly practice manager said, 'The first and only item on my agenda is whether you think we should have the inside and outside of the surgery decorated.'

The two doctors smiled and he asked, 'What's the joke?'

'We're about to start giving my place a facelift in the next few days,' Matthew told him. 'Maybe we ought to see how that works out first. Or have we enough in the kitty to bring in a firm of decorators?'

'Yes, of course,' Douglas replied. 'I wouldn't have suggested it otherwise. We still have some of the money left from the sale of the land at the back of the surgery.' He turned to Henrietta. 'It was before your time, my dear. There was a piece of waste land doing nothing that belonged to the practice, so we sold it, and as you will have seen someone has built a house on it. If you are both agreeable, I will get some estimates from decorating companies and will arrange another meeting when I've got them. Is that all right?'

Yes,' they agreed, and as Douglas got to his feet he said, 'I'll be off, then. My mates at the pub will be waiting for me to join them in a game of snooker.'

When Henrietta went back into the sitting room after seeing him off, Matthew was standing by the window, looking out over the smooth green lawns of The White House, and he said, 'That was short and sweet. We could have sorted it in five minutes back at the practice. I thought Douglas had a list of things to discuss as long as his arm when he asked for a meeting with such urgency, but obviously not. Do you want me to go, too?'

She shook her head. 'Not unless you want to. Let's take our drinks out on to the patio. It's too nice an evening to be indoors.'

He couldn't believe it, Matthew was thinking as they sank down into comfortable wicker chairs. He'd wanted to have Henrietta to himself, and now he'd got his wish, what was he going to do about it? At the surgery they talked freely about practice matters and many other things, but being alone with her here at The White House was a different matter, and in complete contrast to what was in his mind he said, 'Do you ever envy your sister and her husband their lifestyle here?'

'No. I don't. I prefer something more cosy. All I need to be happy and content is love, kindness and integrity.'

'*They* come with a good marriage,' he said sombrely. 'Yet you've never thought of tying the knot.'

'I have, and it wasn't so long ago.'

'What happened if you don't mind my asking?'

Henrietta sighed. 'Our apartments were opposite in the complex where I lived and we were always bumping into each other. He asked me out eventually and we got on well, so much so that I thought something would come of it. But it seemed that he'd been married before. His ex-wife had seen me with him and she came round to tell me that they were divorced and had a little boy who couldn't understand why his daddy never came to see him when he had ample visiting rights.

'I wasn't happy that Miles hadn't told me he'd been

married before. It wouldn't have mattered just as long as he'd told me. But when I asked him why he didn't visit his son, and it turned out that he couldn't be bothered, that was it.'

Matthew nodded. 'It's often a fact of life, Henrietta, that those who have cherish not, and those who have not are left to manage the best they can.' He smiled sadly. 'And speaking of those who have not, I feel I should explain about the perfume you're wearing.'

'I hope you're not going to object to me wearing it in my own time,' she said levelly.

'No. Nothing like that. If you remember, we hadn't known each other more than a couple of days when you wore it the first time, and it threw me. Destination was the perfume Joanna used to wear and instead of explaining I acted the big boss and asked you not to wear it any more at work. I can imagine what you thought of my behaviour that day, as we hadn't exactly hit it off at that time, had we?'

'I would have understood if you'd told me,' she said softly.

'Yes, I know, but I just couldn't get the words out. We'd only just met and the last thing I needed was for you to think I was looking for a shoulder to cry on.'

Henrietta frowned. 'I might have thought it of someone else maybe, but never you. At that time I thought I'd never met a person more in control. I thought you were self-opinionated, brusque and bossy until I saw you with your patients, and had to have a rethink.'

'And what do you think of me now?' he asked in a low voice.

'Er…well…shouldn't the fact that I've offered to help

rejuvenate your house give you some idea?' she said, avoiding a straight answer. 'And by the way Mollie and Keiran can't wait for Saturday to come. They've already sorted out their painting clothes. What are you going to give them to paint?'

'The back gate maybe,' he suggested, and thought that he'd been neatly sidetracked. Maybe it was Henrietta's way of saying she wasn't interested in anything other than their working relationship, and if that was the case, fair enough. On that thought he got up to go.

'Do you want to have a peep at the children before you go?' she asked.

'Yes,' he said immediately, and as he stood looking down at them a few minutes later, rosy and cherubic in sleep, with Henrietta by his side, he was smiling.

'Great kids,' he said, and turning away found himself close up against her. He could smell the perfume again and as if it was the most natural thing in the world he took her in his arms and kissed her, slowly at first and then with rising passion.

After the first moment of surprise Henrietta kissed him back. It was a moment she would have liked to go on and on, but was Matthew just caught up in the past? she wondered, and backed away from him.

It would be the perfume that had made him reach out for her—Joanna's perfume. It must have seemed for a fleeting moment that she was there and she, Henrietta, had become the wife he'd lost.

'I'm sorry, Henrietta,' he said flatly. 'I got carried away. It must have been the perfume and the summer night.'

'And the loneliness,' she said gently.

'Yes, that, too,' he agreed stiffly. Turning, he went, taking the stairs of the wide curving staircase two at time.

When he'd gone Henrietta couldn't settle to anything. After drawing the drapes and setting the alarms, she went to bed, still in a state of disbelief, still with the feeling of Matthew's mouth on hers. If she had been relaxed and at ease when he'd arrived, she certainly was not so now.

Did she want to get involved with a man who was still bound by memories of his dead wife? she asked herself. It would be so easy to love Matthew. He was everything she could want. But would life with him be a continual process of trying to compete with Joanna? Taking second place to a memory?

In a lay-by on the road that led back to his place Matthew had stopped the car and was staring out into the gathering dusk. From the moment Henrietta had opened the door to Douglas and himself, he had wanted her. But he'd known when she'd drawn away from him that she'd thought he was using her. That he was still in love with Joanna and the perfume had brought all the old longings back.

He might have thought that himself until he'd taken her in his arms and kissed her, and it had been then that everything had changed. His feelings for her were new and tender. They had wiped away the dread of being hurt again, but what about Henrietta? Would she want to put her trust in him after the way her previous boyfriend had behaved?

When they'd stood, looking down at the children, for a

mad moment he'd wished that they were theirs, and then for an even crazier moment had presumed that Henrietta was as attracted to him as he was to her.

It had been a stupid thing to do. They had to work together. Before tonight there hadn't been any awkwardness between them, but that would have changed when next they met. Of all the years, months and days he'd been on his own, he had never felt this way about another woman until tonight, and he knew deep down it wasn't going to be the end of it.

The school bus was late turning up the next morning, which meant that Henrietta wasn't on time at the practice. As Matthew watched the clock with a sinking feeling inside him, he was telling himself that she really must be taking a poor view of the previous night's happenings if she wasn't going to put in an appearance.

He had convinced himself that was the case to such an extent that when she came dashing through the front door of the surgery he found himself goggling at her disbelievingly.

'Sorry I'm late,' she gasped. 'The school bus was delayed due to an accident and I couldn't leave the children until I'd seen them safely on it.'

'It's all right,' he assured her. 'Don't worry about it. Just as long as all is well.'

She was moving towards her own room and taking her jacket off at the same time, but she picked up on the question in his voice and turned to look at him. 'If you're referring to what happened last night, yes, all is well, Matthew. I accept that it was just a moment of chemistry that came out of nowhere. That you were missing Joanna, and I don't have any problems with that. As far as I'm concerned, we are still friends.'

For once he was speechless. What Henrietta had just said had stunned him. Joanna had been far from his thoughts when he'd kissed Henrietta. He hadn't been thinking about anyone else, and had wanted it to go on for ever. The feeling of her in his arms and her mouth against his had kindled the kind of desire that he'd almost forgotten existed.

When he'd got home he'd gone upstairs and picked up the photograph from the bedside table. Looking down at it he'd said, 'I'm moving on at last, Joanna. I've met a woman who is bringing light into my life and I know you will be happy for me.'

But this morning that same woman had just told him calmly that she understood why he'd behaved the way he had the previous night and had read nothing into it, treating it as a brief moment of chemistry between the sexes, and there was no way he was going to let her see how much it hurt.

'Fine,' he said, trying to sound casual. 'I'm glad you understood.' And went to start another day of health care.

There was no time for Henrietta to dwell on their conversation as there was a pile of case notes beckoning on her desk and the patients they belonged to would have their eye on the clock in the waiting room. But in the lunch-hour, while Matthew was involved with a salesman from one of the drug companies, her thoughts went back to it.

She had expected him to be relieved at the get-out she'd

given him, but now she wasn't so sure. It hadn't been an easy thing to do. She'd admitted to herself in the long hours of the night that getting to know him had been magical, and if they'd met under other circumstances, without his tragic past casting a shadow over his life, they might have had something very special.

She was happy being part of the practice, happy working and living in the village, and would be happier still if Matthew had a different agenda regarding his private life.

They would be working on his house together at the weekend, and the last thing she wanted was for there to be constraint between them. Hopefully he had understood what she'd said and they would be back to how they had been.

When he surfaced after the meeting with the medical rep he said, 'I called on Dave Lorimer's dad this morning on my way to the surgery. He was out when I stopped by last night.'

He had her attention immediately. 'What did he have to say?'

'Only that he knows all about his son's problems and is very worried. I've phoned Dave to ask him to come to see me out of hours as I'm fully booked for the next few days, and we'll take it from there. But not a lot can be done until he's seen the consultants. I'm going to ring the hospital the first chance I get to see if they've given him an appointment.'

As he turned to go back to his own room he said whimsically, 'Alan asked me if I would be interested in joining the band again.'

'And what did you say.'

'That I would think about it.'

* * *

The sun was high in the sky almost before Henrietta and the children had finished breakfast on Saturday morning, and as she fastened her hair back with a rubber band and planted a baseball cap firmly on top of it, she was looking forward to the day ahead. If Matthew wasn't as attracted to her as she was to him, she was happy just to be in his company, and the children enjoyed being with him almost as much as she did.

The kids were dressed in their old clothes, while she was in a pair of jeans and a well-washed top, and now all they had to do was drive to where he would be waiting for them.

While she was unloading the boot of her car, Mollie and Kieran rushed into the house to find Matthew. Swinging them both up in his arms, he asked, 'So are we ready for a hard day's work?'

He received firm nods and when he looked up Henrietta was standing in the doorway watching them, arms laden with an assortment of paintbrushes, rollers, white spirit and the rest.

He put the children down and told her as he went to take them from her, 'You're looking very businesslike.'

She smiled. 'I'm in charge, remember.'

'All right. But guess what *I've* got. A steam wallpaper stripper!'

Henrietta laughed. 'Well done.'

'So where do you suggest we start?'

'Upstairs and work down maybe. How about tackling the main bedroom first?' she suggested. 'While you're stripping the paper off, I'll sand down the woodwork.'

'Yes, but not in the same room at the same time, I don't

think. A room where a stripper is being used is like a sauna. Sand down the woodwork in another room and then come back to the main bedroom when I've finished.'

'All right,' she agreed amicably. 'But before we go any further, what about our young helpers? What are you going to give them to do?'

'The back gate. There are a couple of brushes and a can of undercoat on the kitchen table for them to make a start.'

'And supposing they make a mess?'

'No problem. There are some old sheets around that Kate has brought. We can put one on the paving near the gate to avoid splashes. By the way, she's also done a bake for us with lots of goodies.'

Picking up the tin of undercoat and a couple of sheets of sandpaper, Matthew took Mollie and Keiran outside to where the back gate stood forlorn and peeling.

They looked up at him questioningly and he said, 'First of all we get rid off all the flaky bits, like this.' And gave the surface of the door a hard rub with the sandpaper. 'When you've done that, tell Henrietta as I'll be up in the bedroom stripping the wallpaper. Then if she thinks you've done a good job she'll show you how to put the undercoat on. Is that OK?'

There was no need to ask. Each with a sheet of sandpaper in their hands they were already on the job.

'Our two young helpers are hard at it,' he told her when he went back inside, 'and will be reporting when they've finished the sanding down.'

He put on a pair of white overalls and reached for the

stripper, 'And you know where I'll be. Give me a shout when it's lunchtime, Henrietta.'

Smiling hazel eyes were observing him from under the peak of the baseball cap. She was happy, and had a feeling that so was he.

CHAPTER SIX

WHEN they stopped for lunch and were all seated around the kitchen table, eating the food that Kate had left for them, Keiran looked across at Matthew and out of the blue said, 'Is your house sad because you haven't got any children?'

Henrietta took a deep breath as she waited for Matthew's reply.

'So you think my house is sad, do you?' he said thoughtfully. 'I suppose it might be happier if children lived here, but children have to have a mother, and there isn't one.'

'Aunt Henny is the same as you. She hasn't got any children either,' Keiran told him. 'She hasn't even got a boyfriend.'

Henrietta placed her hand across her eyes and looked down at the tabletop. She knew where this was leading and was cringing at the thought. 'She says she doesn't want to marry anybody, but we think she would marry you, Uncle Matthew, if you asked her, don't we, Mollie?'

The honorary 'uncle' title had been Henrietta's idea. She'd thought it sounded more respectful than just calling him Matthew, as he'd suggested they should do.

'Yes,' his sister agreed, with dreamy eyes. 'I could be a bridesmaid and scatter rose petals.'

'Yes, and you could also be getting on with painting the back gate,' Henrietta said quickly, getting to her feet. 'Have you both had enough to eat?'

When she looked across at Matthew he was smiling. Leaning over the table, he said in a low voice. 'It's all right. It would seem that matchmakers come in all sizes. But, you know, Henrietta, what Keiran has just said has given me food for thought. He'd picked up on this being a sad house. Children can be so perceptive sometimes. It was a happy place when Joanna was alive and that is how she'd want it to be now. I'm the one who's filled it with gloom, and I've been wrong.'

'I'm so glad that you are beginning to feel like that,' she said quietly.

'I've been feeling it ever since you and the children arrived this morning. There's been noise and laughter in the empty rooms.'

'And the smell of paint?'

He laughed. 'Yes. That's something else that hasn't been there in a long time.' He was flexing his arms and turning to go back to stripping the bedroom, and she thought it would seem that nothing else that Keiran had said had given him food for thought.

Upstairs in the main bedroom Matthew was wondering what Henrietta had thought of the children's suggestion. Not a lot he felt. She had sat with head bent and made no comment, but that didn't mean she hadn't tuned in.

He supposed he could have grasped the opportunity to take it a step further once Mollie and Keiran had gone back to painting the gate, but could imagine how Henrietta would feel at the children having to prod him into action.

The memory of how she'd felt in his arms a couple of nights ago kept coming back. Her slenderness, the low-cut sundress showing lots of pale gold skin and the perfume, familiar yet new on Henrietta, had all made him drop his guard, and there hadn't been a moment since when he hadn't been thinking about her.

When the decorating was finished he was going to take her out as a thank-you gesture and then, without any prodding from Mollie and Keiran, he would tell her how he felt.

By the early evening they'd all had enough. The children had left the painting of the gate and gone inside to watch television, and both Henrietta and Matthew were ready for a rest and a shower.

"I think we'll make tracks,' she told him. 'The children won't need any rocking tonight and neither will I. We'll be back in the morning, and why don't we go out somewhere for a nice lunch to break up the day? You'll know the right places to take them better than I do.'

'Yes, great idea,' he said easily, adding as they walked to the gate, 'I intend to speak to Dave Lorimer tonight and will let you know in the morning what we've talked about.'

She turned to face him and said softly, 'I worked with some clever and dedicated doctors in my last job, but I had to come to a small Cheshire village to find the most caring and the best.

No wonder the people around here hold you in such high regard. I hope you'll be around if ever I need a doctor.'

'So do I,' he told her, and wondered if she would ever want him around in any other guise than that.

The children were tugging at her. It was time to say goodbye until tomorrow, and with the thought of that pleasure to come he waved them off.

As Matthew watched Henrietta and the children getting out of the car on Sunday morning, the good feeling he'd had since the previous day increased.

As he flung open the front door, Mollie and Keiran came running up the drive, happy and bright-eyed after a good night's sleep. Henrietta was close behind looking happy enough but not quite so bright-eyed and rather pale.

'Are you all right?' he asked immediately, picking up on her pallor.

'Yes. I'm fine. I didn't sleep very well, that's all.'

The truth was that she'd hardly slept at all, even though she'd been tired after the day's exertions, and Matthew was the reason. Matthew, who was observing her with the keen glance of the GP and the concerned expression of a friend.

'Was it the thought of coming back here today that kept you awake?' he asked wryly 'Another day's hard grind.'

'No, not at all. There's something therapeutic about watching brightness replace gloom. I enjoyed every moment.'

'Even Kieran's lunchtime chatter?'

'Except for that maybe, which is perhaps best forgotten.'

She knew she must have dozed off at some point during the night as she'd had a crazy dream where she'd been walking down the aisle of the village church in a wedding gown, with Mollie behind her, scattering rose petals.

She'd been able to see the back of the bridegroom waiting for her at the altar, and had known from the set of his shoulders, the cut of his hair and the tanned skin at the back of his neck that it had been Matthew. But when she'd drawn level she'd seen that there had been another woman standing beside him with a smiley mouth and golden hair, and he had been so engrossed in her he hadn't even noticed that she, Henrietta, had been there.

She'd turned to flee and bumped into a man who'd stepped out of the shadows. Miles, the reluctant father. She'd picked up her train and dashed down the aisle like a flash of light with Mollie running behind her, shouting, 'Wait for me, Aunt Henny!'

It had been like dreams often were. A jumble of thoughts connected with recent happenings, mixed up and difficult to comprehend. But as she'd lain wide eyed afterwards it had seemed as if there had been a message of sorts in it. That neither man was meant for *her*. Miles had shown it by just one sentence back there in the city, and as for Matthew, she knew where his heart was in safekeeping. He'd only kissed *her* because she'd smelt like Joanna.

'Aunt Henny hasn't even got a boyfriend,' Keiran had told him in childish concern, and at that moment, sleepless beneath the stars, it had seemed like the most sensible situation to be in.

She'd woken up on Sunday to the sound of church bells pealing out across the green meadows that separated The

White House from the village and had felt the uncertainties that had kept her awake fall away.

When she'd gone to the window to take in the view, as she had each morning, a solitary farmer had been ploughing a field in the distance, and a heron had flown past, bound for the river and its breakfast of some unsuspecting fish.

She wanted to stay in this place for ever, she'd thought, caught in its spell. No matter what else was going on in her life.

But now, with Matthew's dark gaze upon her, she knew that without him in her life the village would be just a delightful place to live. There would be no purpose in her. She was becoming more aware of him all the time, and it wasn't all sexual chemistry.

There was how he was with Mollie and Keiran. They'd taken to him immediately. Then there was the way he ran the practice. She cringed when she thought of how she'd been so critical of everything during her first two days there. She hadn't allowed for his absence and the domestic crisis in John Lomas's life, and hadn't known that Matthew carried a cross of someone else's making.

'There's a place on the edge of town called Barnaby's that the kids would like if we're going out for lunch,' he was saying. 'It isn't what I'd choose for myself, and I don't think their mother would be too chuffed at them eating there, but kids love it. It's a fast-food place. The kind where they serve burgers, french fries and milkshakes.'

She smiled. 'They'll think that's great. And as for my sister, she *is* a loving mother, you know. A bit overpowering,

I admit, but I'm sure they'll have been to that kind of place before, even though Pamela would shudder at the thought.'

Together they gathered up some brushes and rolls of wallpaper and headed up the stairs. 'By the way, Matthew, what about David Lorimer?'

'Oh, yes. You were right about him having the symptoms of a brain tumour,' he said. 'I examined him and we had a chat. His blood pressure was a bit high, but that could be because of the stress that he's under. We need some fast action there, Henrietta. Tomorrow we start pushing for that appointment.'

'I feel better now that you've seen him,' she said soberly. 'He's been on my mind all the time.

As predicted, the children did like Barnaby's and loved the burgers, fries and milkshakes. So did the two doctors. An old lady sitting nearby, tucking into a cheeseburger, said, 'You have two bonny children. The girl is like you,' she said to Matthew, 'and the boy like his mother.'

Henrietta watched Keiran's mouth open as he prepared to put her right and said quickly, 'Shush, Keiran.'

Unaware of her mistake, the lady said, 'I've come to do some shopping with my friends. We come on Sundays as it's quieter, but when we're ready for a bite they won't come into this place. They want tablecloths and plates and fancy cakes. I say, give me a burger any time.'

When she'd gone, leaning heavily on a stick, Matthew said, 'We've just been paired off again. Do people see something about us that we don't. Or are they just too quick to assume?'

'I've no idea,' she replied distantly, with the memory of Margot Chilton's *faux pas* surfacing. 'And does it matter?'

She wasn't smiling, as he'd thought she might have done, and he wondered if Henrietta was telling him in a roundabout sort of way that she couldn't care less about having her name coupled with his, as she wasn't interested anyway.

If that was the case, how would she feel if she knew that when he'd arrived home on the night he'd kissed her, he'd told Joanna he was letting go. That he'd finally found someone just as special as she'd been and, though he would never forget her, he was moving on.

In his own way and his own time, he was going to tell Henrietta that, and the last thing he wanted when the moment came was for her to think that he'd been spurred on by everyone coupling them together.

For the rest of Sunday they worked in silence as they painted and papered the bedrooms, while Mollie and Keiran, unaware of any atmosphere, worked industriously on the back gate, a lot more interested now that they were putting on the final coat of green paint.

The finished article would be far from perfect, but neither of the two doctors were bothered about that. From Henrietta's point of view, it was doing them no harm to do something for someone else and as for Matthew he was just happy to have them around.

When it was time for them to go he went out to the car to say goodbye, and as he and Henrietta faced each other he said, 'Thanks for giving up your weekend, Henrietta. If ever you decide to buy a place of your own in the village, I'll do the same for you should it be necessary.'

So he wasn't contemplating asking her to settle down under his roof, she thought, and told him breezily, 'You don't have to do anything in return. We'll come again next weekend...if you want us.'

'Of course I do. I've been wondering if you'd come round some time to choose carpets and curtains with me. One of the big stores has a facility where their experts will come out with swatches of different fabrics for you to choose from, and will advise generally.'

'Yes. I don't mind doing that,' she told him in the same breezy tone, 'but how? We're at the practice all day, and in the evenings I'm housebound because of the children.'

'I could come up to The White House.'

'Er...yes...I suppose you could,' she agreed, with the memory as clear as crystal of the last time he'd done that. But she wasn't expecting any repeat performances.

It was obvious that Matthew had no yearnings in her direction if he found it so offputting when they kept being seen as a couple. That being so, there was no way he was going to find out that she was falling in love with him.

In the week that followed David Lorimer went for the tests to see if he might have a brain tumour and they proved positive. From the checking of hormone levels in the blood and urine, a CT scan and an MRI, he was diagnosed with a pituitary tumour. That was the bad news that threw Dave and his family into a state of despair. But there was some light in the darkness, and Matthew was pleased to see how positive Dave was being when he came to surgery.

'The consultant told me he would have to operate to remove the tumour, otherwise it would grow and press on other areas of my brain,' Dave explained. 'He was pleased to hear about the baby, as he said the tumour would also affect my fertility if it was left. If it had been more advanced, we might have found it difficult to conceive as my sperm count would have been too low.' The young man smiled. 'He also told me that pituitary tumours are almost invariably benign, and as long as no hiccups present themselves during surgery, I should make a good recovery. I cried like a baby when he told me,' he admitted.

'I'm not surprised,' Matthew said. 'How soon is he going to operate?'

'Some time in the next couple of weeks. The sooner the better. Those at home are feeling a lot happier and so am I. I've been teasing my dad, telling him that he was only worried because he thought he was going to be one short in the band.' And with that he went on his way, back to those who loved him.

When Dave had gone Matthew went to tell Henrietta the outcome of her concerns over him, and as he was leaving her consulting room he said, 'Would Friday night be all right for the people from the store to come round? You haven't got anything planned?'

'No. that would be fine. The children still go to bed early on Friday nights, even though there's no school on Saturday. They're always tired at the end of the week. So, as I mentioned before, I'm always at home in the evenings.'

'And it doesn't bother you, having no social life?'

'No, not really. There is plenty of room for me to spread myself around in The White House, and if I had to go somewhere in the evening there is no one I would trust to be with the children, apart from Kate and yourself, and I feel that she's been here long enough by the time I get home.'

'Which just leaves me.'

'Yes, and as far as Mollie and Keiran are concerned you would be number-one choice in any case. But I'm not likely to be going anywhere so the necessity won't arise.'

There was still a coolness between them after Sunday, he thought, but neither of them were going to let it interfere with practice matters.

The salesperson from the department store was due to arrive at eight o'clock on Friday evening and Matthew was early. The children had only just settled down for the night when Henrietta opened the door to him and put her finger to her lips.

'Don't let Mollie or Keiran hear your voice or they'll be downstairs in a flash,' she whispered.

'Well, it is Saturday tomorrow, you know.'

'Yes, I do know, but if you want me to concentrate on what this person is saying, I don't want the children to come romping down the stairs all set for fun and games with you.'

She wondered if he really did need her input for his refurbishing, or if it was just an excuse to see the children and he was disappointed they weren't around.

'So, what sort of a colour scheme do you think I should choose?' he asked, as if reading her thoughts. He was looking down at the carpet beneath his feet, a thick pile of the palest cream, and commented. 'Nothing as pale as this, I think.'

'Why not?' Henrietta wanted to know. 'There'll be only you to walk on it.'

'At present maybe, but supposing my life changed and I wasn't the only one living there?'

Henrietta ignored the painful jolt she felt at his words. After all, here was a man who didn't like being manipulated. Who wasn't happy at the way his name kept being linked with hers. Which made it look pretty certain that it wouldn't be her feet walking on a pale cream carpet.

A ring on the doorbell announced the curtain and carpet person had arrived and for the next couple of hours they were engrossed in colours and quality.

'Do you think pale green carpets and gold for the curtains would go with the decorating we've got planned?' Matthew asked, and she nodded.

'It would be perfect. Once it's finished, your house will be so beautiful you won't ever want to leave it.'

'That would depend on who I was sharing it with.'

Henrietta felt her spirits take a further dive. There it was again, the hint that Matthew was well and truly out of the doldrums, and she might have to stand by and watch the transformation. She could feel the maiden aunt mantle settling on her shoulders already.

It was ten o'clock and the satisfied salesman had left with a large order in his book, and they had been left with the promise that fitting would take place whenever it was requested, as long as they allowed three weeks for the order to be processed.

When Henrietta went back into the sitting room after seeing him off Matthew said, 'So are we on line for the decorating again tomorrow? I'm really getting into the swing of things now. I can't wait to see the result, and it's all thanks to you, Henrietta. You've done what no one else could do, made me see sense.'

She managed a smile. 'I'm only glad to see you happier, Matthew, and, yes, we'll be round tomorrow. What are you going to have the children doing now they've finished the gate?'

'Are you sure they'll want to paint again? The novelty will have worn off by now. They can play in the garden if they want, or watch television.'

She wanted him to go. He was only inches away. She could smell his aftershave and see the creases around the dark eyes that she sometimes felt saw into her mind. Yet if that was the case he would know that she loved him. That *she* wanted to be the one who was going to live in the transformed house with him. But Matthew wasn't the only one who had his pride. So, prolonging the agony, she said. 'How about a coffee before you go?' and hoped he would refuse.

He didn't. Instead, he came into the kitchen and watched her as she made it, and then carried the two mugs into the sitting room while she followed with a plate of pastries.

He had seated himself opposite her, so wasn't so near as before. She began to relax until he said, 'The children were telling me last week that they have a school trip next Saturday. That they're all going to the Fylde coast for the day.'

'Yes, that's right. They will be picked up here in the village at eight o'clock in the morning and dropped off at half-seven in the evening. I can still turn up for the deco-rating, though.'

He shook his head. 'No such thing. We'll give the deco-rating a miss and spend the day together once morning surgery is over. Just think, Henrietta, no patients, no deco-rating and, delightful as they are, no children. There *will* be one thing, though. I'm down for playing cricket on the village green in the afternoon. How would you feel about that.'

'All of it sounds lovely, as long as I haven't got anything else planned,' she told him, happy at the thought of being with him but not too chuffed about being taken so much for granted.

He was frowning. 'I'm sorry. I should have remem-bered that you have a life of your own, just as I do. I hope you'll forgive me.'

She smiled across at him. 'There's nothing to forgive. I'd love to spend the day with you.'

The frown disappeared as quickly as it had come. 'So how about once you've seen the children off and I've done the surgery, I call for you and we go into town to do some shopping, then have lunch somewhere, followed by me putting on my whites and trying to hit ball with bat, or al-ternatively knock somebody's bails off. Kate will be there. She's one of the ladies who see to the refreshments in the cricket pavilion.'

'That all sounds delightful,' she told him, her spirits rising again. 'Just as long as there isn't anyone else you would rather spend the time with.'

What was that supposed to mean? he wondered. What had he said to make her think that?

'There isn't,' he said firmly, and got up to go. At the front door he turned. 'What are the security arrangements like at this place?'

'Exactly what you would expect,' she told him. 'First class. Security lights all over the grounds, an alarm system inside the house with sensors and panic buttons wherever I look. Why do you ask?'

'Henrietta, why do you think? Make sure you set it all in motion when I've gone.'

'Of course,' she told him calmly, and as he went striding out to his car she was thinking that if Matthew was as concerned about what made her happy as he was about what kept her safe, she would be content.

As he drove the short distance home Matthew was thinking that it had been time well spent for sorting out his furnishings, and as far as he and Henrietta were concerned it had not been an evening of lost opportunities. The thought of just the two of them spending some time together seemed to have appealed to her as much as it had to him. Yet he sensed that she was still wary of him.

Was she afraid of being second in his life after Joanna? he wondered. He should have reassured her about that, but would look somewhat foolish if the problem didn't arise and she wasn't that attracted to him.

Maybe a whole day with just the two of them would help make their feelings towards each other clearer, and until then he would count the days. Though before that there was tomorrow, *and* working together at the practice during the next week, but it was the thought of having her to himself that gave him the most pleasure.

* * *

Dave Lorimer didn't have to wait long for surgery. He was sent for within the week, much to the relief of all concerned. His father came into the surgery on the day after the operation and told Matthew, 'They've removed the tumour and my lad's in Intensive Care, getting over the operation. Now we're waiting to hear if it was benign, as none of us are going to relax until we know for certain. We're so grateful for the way the practice picked up on it so quickly.'

'You have Dr Mason to thank for that,' Matthew told him. The same Dr Mason who is helping me decorate my house, looking after her sister's children and doing a good job here, but is keeping me at a distance when it comes to anything else, he thought.

'Will you thank her for us, then?' Alan said. 'And what about the band, Matthew? When are you coming back? A cheer will go up if you ever walk through the door of the Scout hut again. There isn't anyone in the village who doesn't want to see you back to how you used to be.'

Matthew smiled. 'I'm working on it by making a start with the cricket team on Saturday. As for the band, give me time. I don't even know where my trombone is.'

He wasn't going to tell Alan that he was working on it from another angle that really would bring him out into the light if he didn't make a mess of it.

After Alan had gone, Matthew went outside to make a start on his home visits and found Henrietta standing by her car, about to set off to do the same thing, looking cool and composed in a smart dress of brown linen and a cream jacket.

When he saw her, Matthew wanted to go across and take her in his arms. Shatter her calm with his mouth on hers and her body hard up against his chest. But it was not the time or place. Instead, he gave a casual wave in her direction and went to where his own car was parked.

She was still standing there when he drew level and, rolling down the window, he said, 'Dave Lorimer has had the op and is in Intensive Care. That's the latest bulletin. And about us. Are we still on for Saturday?'

'Er…no…I mean yes.'

'Good. Though you don't sound so sure.'

'Yes. I am. I'm looking forward to it.'

In truth she was and she wasn't. Because she didn't know what was in his mind. It would be very different from a day spent painting and papering, where half the time they weren't in the same room. They would have each other's undivided attention. As Matthew had said when he'd suggested it, no children, no patients, no decorating. Just a few hours to themselves.

Once he was out of sight she set off on her rounds, the first name on her list that of an elderly man who lived in a stone cottage beside a disused waterwheel at the far end of the village.

Long ago, in the eighteenth century, wheels like it had been used to fashion some of the tools needed in the making of the Peak Forest Canal. But now it lay unused, bypassed by the fast-flowing river as it came down from the hills. Thomas Saxby lived with the sound of running water for ever in his ears. But it wasn't his ears that were bothering him.

He came to the door leaning heavily on a stick, and by way of introduction said, 'I was watching two kingfishers having a fight by the river bank last night and it was muddy underfoot. I slipped and went down on my back and it's been hurting ever since, Doctor. By the way, who are you? Where's Dr Cazalet? He isn't poorly or anything like that, is he? I'm told that he's been in Pakistan.'

'Yes, he has and, no, he isn't poorly,' Henrietta said. 'He's been back for a few weeks now. I'm the new doctor at the practice.

'Aye, well, I don't get to hear much of what goes on in the village these days.'

'Do you think you can manage to get your shirt off, Mr Saxby, and perhaps loosen your trousers around the waist?

After she'd felt all over his back with practised fingers, Henrietta said, 'There is some bruising just above the bottom of your spine, but I don't think you've damaged anything. I'll drop a prescription off at the chemist for some gel that will take away the inflammation and soreness, and will come back to see you in a few days. If it should get worse before then, send for me immediately and I will arrange for an X-ray.'

'Aye, all right, Doctor, but how am I going to get the prescription? You've seen the state I'm in and the chemist is at the other end of the village.'

'You don't have to worry as they'll deliver it for you, Mr Saxby.'

The old man sighed in relief. 'Really! That's wonderful. When you get back to the surgery, remember me to Dr Cazalet, will you? They were a lovely couple, Matthew and that wife of his.'

'Yes. I'll do that,' she replied, and thought that it was

only natural that the lovely Joanna should be remembered by the locals. But it was a reminder that she, Henrietta, was the newcomer, on the fringe of village life. Maybe one day she wouldn't feel like that if she put down roots there, but would she want to be around if Matthew didn't want her?

CHAPTER SEVEN

'I SAW Thomas Saxby this morning,' Henrietta told Matthew when they met up at lunchtime. 'He sends his regards.'

'What was the matter with Tom?'

'He'd slipped in mud on the river bank and strained his back.'

'Badly?'

'Not at a first glance. I've prescribed some gel to take away the soreness and told him to get back to me if there's no improvement in a couple of days.'

'He's a great old guy. Tom used to take me birdwatching when I was a kid.'

She smiled. 'It must have been like paradise, living in this place as a child.'

'It still is, in spite of everything.'

'Are your parents alive?' she asked, and his face clouded over.

'My mother died when I was in my teens. My father remarried and went to live abroad. He wanted me to go with him, but I opted to live with Kate. We send each other cards at Christmas and birthdays and that's about it. So it was just Kate and I, until you came along, level-headed, impersonal, no axe to grind, and began to bring me back into the real world.'

She was tempted to tell him that there was nothing impersonal in her feelings for him, that when she was near him she was far from level-headed, but he was asking, 'What about *your* parents. Where are they?'

'Gone. My parents died in a motorway pile-up when Pamela was twenty-two and I was seventeen. She took charge of everything and was there for me all the time I was at medical college. Those are the kinds of situations where she functions best—crisis times.

'By the time I'd graduated she had married Charles and we weren't so close as before, but we've always kept in touch. When she had the children I was hooked. So there you have the uninteresting story of my life. Make of it what you will.'

'One thing is clear,' he said flatly. 'Neither of us have spent a great deal of time within the circle of a loving family. I had every intention of making up for that when I married Joanna, but that was not to be either. Yet in the middle of all my misery there has always been Kate, caring and faithful.'

'She's wonderful,' Henrietta told him. 'The children love her, and I can relax while I'm at the practice, knowing that she's with them. Has she never married?'

'No. There have been a few after her, but she doesn't seem interested in anyone she's met so far. I've told her a thousand times that I don't want to put a blight on her love life, but she just laughs.'

She didn't know whether he was blighting his aunt's love life, but it wouldn't take much for him to blight hers, she thought wryly. When they'd first met she hadn't even liked him, but as the days had passed that had changed as she'd got to know his worth as a doctor and a man, and now he was never out of her thoughts.

'People who aren't used to being part of a family usually think in one of two ways,' he said, breaking into her thoughts. 'They either become self-sufficient loners, or at the first opportunity fill the gap in their lives with a family of their own because they long for that kind of love. Which category would you say we come into?'

'A bit of both, I suppose,' she said hesitantly, not sure where the question was leading. 'I've had to stand on my own two feet since my teens, but I intend to marry and have children one day.' She went on laughingly, 'If only to put Mollie and Keiran's minds at rest. I'll not forget in a hurry Keiran's anxiety when he told you that I hadn't even got a boyfriend. But I can cope with it, just as long as he doesn't advertise for someone in the post office window.'

He joined in her laughter. 'I have to say I felt for you that day, especially as he was trying to get us both off the shelf in one go. But, as I've said before, I do like to make my own decisions.'

'And so do I, just in case you've forgotten,' she said promptly, and on that note she went to get ready for the second surgery of the day with the feeling that she'd just been warned off.

Matthew sighed. His feelings for Henrietta were like tender new shoots coming out of dark earth, he thought.

She was nothing like Joanna, and that was how he wanted it to be. But he wished he knew how *she* felt about him…

They were both kept busy for the rest of the day and it wasn't until she was driving home in the late afternoon that Henrietta's thoughts went back to their conversation in the lunch-hour.

They had so much in common. No parents to strengthen family bonds. Both of them doctors who loved children. Each of them equally enchanted by the Cheshire country-side. And yet they weren't getting any closer.

'What's wrong?' Kate asked when Henrietta walked into the kitchen where she was clearing up after the children's meal.

'Er, nothing,' she told her unconvincingly.

Kate was not to be sidetracked. 'It's Matthew, isn't it? Do you have feelings for him?'

Henrietta sighed, too disheartened to sidestep the question. 'Yes, Kate, I do. But, please, I beg of you, don't ever let Matthew find out. The children have been trying to marry us off to each other. Various other people have thought us to be a couple and he doesn't like it.'

Kate sighed, too. 'That man is dear to my heart, but he must be blind if he can't see what's under his nose here at The White House.'

Henrietta's smile was wry. 'Then blind he must be, Kate.'

When she drew back the drapes on Saturday morning warm summer rain was coming down in torrents out of a leaden sky.

That was the first blight of the day. The second was

when Mollie woke up with a temperature and was sick after her breakfast, which meant that a coach ride to the coast was not going to be a good idea.

When Henrietta explained gently that there was going to be no outing for her, the little girl dissolved into tears and wouldn't be consoled when Keiran promised to bring her back a stick of Blackpool rock.

He was still raring to go, but she had to get him to the coach, and Mollie was still nauseous and fretful. If she had to watch it set off without her there really would be tears. It was just seven o'clock and there was only one person she could ask to collect him and take him to the pick-up point in the village.

She rang Matthew on the phone beside the little girl's bed, and when he answered and heard her voice with Mollie's sobs in the background, he said anxiously, 'Henrietta! What's wrong?'

'I'm sorry to disturb you,' she said.

Before she could say anything else he said, 'Is that Mollie I can hear crying?'

'Yes, she's not well. She's just been sick and has a temperature, so she won't be going on the outing. But Keiran is fine, and I'm phoning to ask if you wouldn't mind picking him up from here and seeing him safely onto the coach.'

'Yes, of course I will,' he said immediately. 'What time do you want me there?'

'A quarter to eight, if that's all right.'

'Yes. I'll be there.'

'I'm sorry that our plans for the day are going to have to be cancelled,' she said regretfully.

'It's no big deal. First things first, and a sick child always comes first,' he said briskly, concealing his disappointment. 'I'll be with you shortly.'

So their day together had been 'no big deal', she thought glumly. Why had he suggested it, then?

When she went upstairs to check on Mollie, she was sniffling into a tissue. 'I'm so disappointed, Aunt Henny,' she said tearfully.

'Yes, I know you are,' Henrietta said gently as she cuddled her niece. Disappointment seemed to be the order of the day, but only as far as she and Mollie were concerned. Keiran was still on track with the school outing, and Matthew hadn't sounded as if cancelling their day out had mattered all that much.

As he drove to The White House at just gone half past seven Matthew was thinking that the day so far was in keeping with the weather. Rain was still lashing down out of a steel-grey sky, instead of the sunkissed mornings they'd been getting of late.

He saw that the river wasn't dawdling over a shallow, rocky bed, as it had during the dry weather, but was bounding along beneath the pouring rain. Up above, the peaks were shrouded in the mist that could come down so quickly when the weather changed.

His mood was like the day, he thought. Obviously he was concerned about young Mollie, but couldn't help feeling disappointed that the time he'd planned to spend with Henrietta wasn't going to happen.

He'd made light of it when she'd phoned him for her

sake. It was difficult enough for her, one of the children being ill while she was looking after them, without her having a guilt trip about their arrangements being cancelled.

When he arrived Keiran was ready with spending money and a packed lunch, and raring to be off. 'I'll pick him up at seven o'clock when the coach gets back in case you are still housebound with Mollie,' he said. 'Where is she?'

'Still in bed. She's sleeping now and seems cooler, but I'm not going to be taking my eyes off her. Do you think I should tell Pamela that she's not well if she phones?'

'I wouldn't mention it unless she gets worse. Your sister is far away and it would be a shame to alarm her unduly.'

She was wearing the silk robe and nightdress that she'd worn the night the cows had come, and in her present harassed state wasn't aware of how desirable she looked.

'We've got a few moments before we need to set off,' he said, bringing his thoughts back to the matter in hand. 'Let me see Mollie before I go. A second opinion always comes in handy.'

As she led him up the wide curving staircase Henrietta caught a glimpse of herself in a mirror and shuddered at the reflection that looked back at her. Hair tangled, dark smudges beneath her eyes, having been awake most of the night thinking about him, and dressed only in the flimsy lingerie that would normally only be seen by herself.

He felt Mollie's pulse and then carefully placed his hand on her temples, and when she saw the gentleness in his glance as he looked down at the sleeping child, Henrietta knew that if she ever had children she would want him to be their father.

'She feels cool enough now,' he said, 'but give me a ring if anything else develops. I don't want you to have to face this worry on your own.'

'I don't want to break into your day again if I can help it,' she told him. 'You've already offered to pick Keiran up this evening. If Mollie is well enough, I'll collect him myself. I'll let you know if I'm going to do that.'

'Do you have to be so damned independent?' he said tightly. 'I'm trying to help, as I would for anyone in this sort of situation caring for children.'

He turned to Keiran, who was more than ready to go. 'Let's be off, then, shall we, Keiran? Say goodbye to Henrietta.' And taking Keiran's hand in his, the man and boy went down the winding staircase together.

The rain had cleared by the middle of the morning and the sun had returned, warm and welcoming. And even more cheering, Mollie was much better by lunchtime. Whatever it was that had been wrong with her, it seemed to have cleared. Her temperature had gone down and she was no longer feeling sick.

And as a brighter picture presented itself Henrietta wondered how they could spend the rest of the day that had started so badly. She was longing to see Matthew again. After he'd sent Keiran off safely he would have gone to do the Saturday surgery and what then? Maybe he'd stuck to their original plan and gone into town for lunch. After the early morning phone call she didn't want to ring him again. Yet he would be wondering how Mollie was and she wanted him to know that she was better.

There was the cricket match that was to take place on the village green, she thought, if the turf wasn't too saturated after the rain. It was one place where she would be sure to find him. She could watch the cricket while Mollie played. It wouldn't exactly be the prime time together that they'd planned, with half the village on the team and the other half watching, but at least she would be where she could see him.

Apart from taking the surgery Matthew hadn't been anywhere. After it was over he'd gone home and spent the rest of the morning painting. He was upset that Henrietta wouldn't let him help. He was always there to sort out the troubles of the rest of the village, but when it came to the one who really mattered she didn't want to know. Yet he was the one she'd phoned early that morning, so what had changed since then?

When he'd gone upstairs he'd seen his cricket whites laid out neatly on the bed and thought wryly that Kate must have decided that after lying unused for so long a wash and press was required. The way the day was going it looked as if the match was going to be the only thing not cancelled, subject to the pitch not being waterlogged.

When he arrived the general activity told him that it wasn't and he smiled. Bails were being placed on stumps. Food and drinks were being carried into the pavilion for those requiring refreshments, and the seating around the village green was filling up.

He wouldn't be there if it wasn't for Henrietta, he

thought. Not because she'd persuaded him to play again. She hadn't known he had, but getting to know her had changed his life. Made him want a new start, and he wished she could be there.

When he looked up she was standing on the boundary, holding Mollie by the hand, and he had to look again to make sure he wasn't seeing things. Then he strode across to them, smiling his pleasure, looking down at Mollie and asking, 'Am I to take it that we have a recovery?'

Henrietta was smiling back. 'It would appear so.'

'That's great. You are the last two people I was expecting to see here. Are you sure you won't be bored?'

'No. I won't be bored. How could I be?' she said softly. 'It will be wonderful watching you getting back into village life again.'

He reached out and traced his fingers gently across her cheek. 'We both know who I have to thank for that, don't we?' he said, happy that whatever had been upsetting her earlier seemed to have gone.

They were calling him over to the pavilion as the match was about to start and he said, 'I'll have to go. I'm one of the opening bats. Heaven knows why. I'm so out of practice it just isn't true.'

As he walked to the crease the answer was there. Everyone present—players, spectators and those preparing the food—began to clap. It went on for minutes until someone shouted, 'Welcome back, Doc.' He raised his bat in salute, and the game began.

Henrietta's eyes were awash with tears. She hoped that if Joanna could see him she would be as happy for him as she was. Matthew deserved so much better than the life he'd been living in bitterness and solitude. He'd made the breakthrough and she knew that, whatever happened between the two of them, he wouldn't go back to it.

Kate had seen them and she came across exclaiming, 'Why, if it isn't young Mollie! Are you feeling better?'

'Yes, thank you,' the little girl said, and with her glance on what was going on inside the pavilion she asked, 'Can I help you while Aunt Henny watches the cricket?'

'Yes, of course you can, darling,' Kate told her, and off they went.

As the afternoon progressed Henrietta was at peace as she watched the game and took in the beautiful setting where it was being played. After the rain the grass was a lush green and against it the white sight screen and players' clothes really stood out.

At the other side of the village green was the river and a row of limestone cottages standing out agelessly beneath the darker greens and blacks of the peaks now that the mist had gone.

It was England at its most beautiful, she thought, and as Matthew flashed her a smile before he hit a ball to the boundary, she knew that the fates had brought her there for a reason and it was only a few feet away. They were meant for each other, if only he could see it.

The game was over by half past six, which gave Henrietta ample time to meet the school coach to collect Keiran, and while she was waiting to say goodbye to Matthew when he came out of the changing room, she was chatting to Kate.

'It was a shame that your day was spoilt,' Kate said. 'I could come up one night if you like, while Matthew takes you somewhere nice to make up for today. Shall I suggest it to him?'

'Suggest what to me?' his voice said from behind, before Henrietta could reply.

'That I mind the children one night while you take Henrietta out to make up for today.'

'Good idea. What does she say?'

'Nothing so far, but she might do if we let her get a word in edgeways.'

Henrietta smiled. 'That would be lovely if you're in favour of the idea,' she told him. 'It would be my first night out since moving here.'

'That's settled, then. If you choose a time, I'll make the arrangements.' He smiled. 'Before you go, how did you like the cricket?'

'I enjoyed it immensely.'

A voice from nearby butted in at that moment and it turned out to be that of Alan Lorimer. 'All Matthew needs now is to find his trombone and he's back on course.'

'Not quite,' Matthew replied. 'There's still something missing.'

'It was great, Aunt Henny,' Keiran said on their way home from the pick-up point. 'We made sand castles, paddled, went on the Pleasure Beach, had donkey rides and lots of other things.'

Mollie was in the back seat of the car and Henrietta cautioned in a low voice, 'You'd better not tell Mollie all of that. Or the tears will be back when she hears what she's missed. Have you brought her any rock?'

'Yes, I've brought two sticks, a pink one and a green one.'

They arrived home and Mollie was delighted when Keiran produced the rock.

'Can I have some now?' she asked hopefully.

'Yes. You can have a small piece, but not too much. Remember you were sick this morning.' Henrietta told her.

Eventually both the children were asleep. Mollie was back to her normal self and sleeping peacefully when Henrietta left her to supervise Keiran's bathtime, and once he was cleaned up and had enjoyed a sleepy cuddle on her knee, he too was soon in dreamland.

As the house settled into quietness Henrietta sank down on to the sofa in the sitting room and closed her eyes. When she opened them again the light had gone. The sun was setting on the horizon and the phone on the table beside her was ringing.

'Henrietta, it's me,' Matthew said. 'Is everything all right. It took you a long time to answer.'

'Yes, we're all right,' she told him. 'I'd just fallen asleep after putting the kids to bed. Mollie seems fine now and Keiran went out like a light after all the sun and sea air at Blackpool. Apparently they had a much better day weatherwise then we did.'

She was conscious that she was making conversation and knew it was because she was so happy to hear his voice. 'It's kind of you to phone,' she told him.

'Kind! What do you mean "kind". We're friends, aren't we?'

'Yes.'

'And the mainstays in a top-notch medical practice?'

'Yes.'

'So, I'm doing what I would do for anyone I care for, if you get my drift.'

She didn't get his drift at all. Didn't want to if it meant that she was just one of many.

'I have to go,' he was saying. 'I've just got back from my Saturday meal at the Goose and am going round to Daniel's for a couple of hours to play chess, darts or whatever he fancies. Remember you have my mobile number if you need me.'

'Yes, thanks,' she said softly. 'Enjoy yourself with Daniel and say hello for me.' With the warm feeling of having someone caring about her wellbeing, she went upstairs to bed, thinking that it had been a day of ups and downs. Thankfully with more ups than downs.

On Monday morning Matthew's first question was, 'How's Mollie?'

'She's fine,' Henrietta told him. 'I've just seen them both off to school and she seems back to normal.'

His second question was, 'Where do you want to go when we have this evening out?'

'I don't mind,' she told him tranquilly. It was enough that such an event was about to happen, she thought.

'The theatre maybe, and then a meal afterwards?'

'I'd love to go to the theatre. But a show and then a meal would make us very late back and we would be keeping Kate from her bed. It's good of her to offer to stay with

Mollie and Keiran, but I don't want to impose on her kindness. Why don't we go to the Goose? The restaurant will be open on weeknights, won't it?'

'Yes, I would imagine so, but if we decide to go there, why don't we go on a Saturday? Then we won't have the surgery to face the next morning.'

'Yes, of course,' she agreed, 'but you don't have to feel that you've got to make it up to me for the Saturday just gone. It wasn't all disappointments. Mollie soon recovered. The sun came out *and* there was the cricket. Flashes of white on green, and the thud, clonk and sprint as the batter hit the ball.'

He was smiling. 'Wow! You *were* impressed.'

She smiled back. 'Everything about this place impresses me.' You in particular, she thought.

'So do I take it that you'll join me at my usual table at the Goose next Saturday night?'

She nodded. 'Yes, you do.'

'Fine. I'll warn them that it will be two instead of one, and hope that there won't be any clapping there when they see me with a lady for the first time ever. I've only gone there since I lost Joanna.'

'People really do care about you, Matthew. It brought tears to my eyes when they clapped you on to the pitch at the cricket match. It was such a touching moment,' she told him.

He gave a wry smile. 'I'm sure there must have been those there who thought my return to sensible living was not before time. But they're kind people. Most of them at the cricket were friends that I'd shut out of my life while I was grieving, and had eventually given up on me.

'And as for you, Henrietta, I don't ever want anything connected with me to make you cry. I want you to be happy and content. I just hope I can make you feel like that.'

At that moment one of the receptionists appeared, calling for help, and the two doctors hurried to where a middle-aged woman was lying on the floor in front of Reception.

There was a film of perspiration on her face and her lips were blue. 'It looks as if we have a heart attack on our hands,' he said, as he knelt beside the unconscious woman.

Henrietta checked the woman's tongue wasn't blocking her airway and she nodded.

'Ring for an ambulance,' Matthew told the receptionist, 'and close the waiting-room door while we're attending to the patient. We don't want an audience.'

'It's only eight o'clock,' she reminded him. 'There's no one in there so far.'

'Right. Well, when they come, redirect them in through the back door. So what happened with this lady?'

Henrietta was unbuttoning the cotton blouse the patient was wearing while Matthew checked her pulse and heartbeat.

'This is Valerie Seddon. She came in to make an appointment. She's new in the area and hasn't been on our list for long,' the receptionist said. 'We were chatting when suddenly she clutched at her chest, started fighting for breath, and then collapsed.'

'She's still breathing,' Matthew told Henrietta, 'but it's very shallow. These first moments with a cardiac arrest are so important. We need the ambulance fast.'

'It was chest pains that she'd come about,' he was told.

'Not without cause, it would seem. They'll check for arrhythmia once she's on the coronary unit and if there is anything of that nature, treatment can begin immediately, but delay can be fatal. We might have to resuscitate her.'

A car door slammed outside and a fast-response doctor came racing in, carrying oxygen equipment. 'Have we still got a pulse?' he asked, dropping to his knees beside the two doctors.

'Just about,' Matthew told him.

'Good.' He started to give the patient oxygen. 'This should help. The ambulance wasn't far behind me.'

'Have we an address for Ms Seddon?' Matthew asked, and the receptionist scribbled it down for him.

'There is only one better place to collapse than in a doctor's surgery, and it's inside the hospital,' the fast-response doctor commented as the sound of the ambulance sirens broke into the peace of the countryside.

'That was a good start to the week,' Henrietta said soberly when the ambulance had set off for A and E with all speed with Valerie Seddon, and the fast-response medic had gone to his next urgent callout.

'There could be someone waiting at home who is going to be getting anxious if she doesn't show up. Shall I ask the staff to phone to see if there's anyone there?'

'No. I'll do it myself,' Matthew said. 'Her relatives will feel more reassured if I talk to them and explain exactly what happened and that she's on her way to hospital.'

The waiting room had been filling up with patients coming in the back way and casting curious glances at what was going on at the other end of the passage, and he said,

'If you'll get started on the morning surgery, I'll make the phone call and then join you.'

There *had* been a husband expecting his wife back from the surgery, and when Matthew phoned the number that was on Valerie Seddon's record card, Mr Seddon listened to what he had to say in dismay.

Then the man had rallied and said, 'Thank you, Dr Cazalet, for letting me know. I'll set off for A and E immediately.'

'How many times has that happened? A patient being sent to hospital straight from the surgery?' Henrietta questioned when they were having a coffee and a sandwich before setting off on the house calls.

'More times than you'd think,' he told her. 'We've had to send for the ambulance when someone has collapsed from over-anxiety or delayed in coming to see us until whatever problem they had was so serious they were taken ill on the premises.'

'That poor man! Receiving that kind of news out of the blue.'

'Yes, but what about his wife? She's the one we should be sorry for. Let's hope she's responding to the treatment they're giving her.'

CHAPTER EIGHT

NOTHING was going to stop him from taking Henrietta out on Saturday night, Matthew vowed as the days went by. When he'd told Alan at the match that there was still something missing in his life, he'd been watching her expression and been disappointed because it had told him nothing.

He might be back on the cricket team, had felt a stirring of interest in the band, and was sprucing his house up with Henrietta's help, but none of it would mean anything if she didn't feel the same as he did.

Until she'd come into his life he'd intended being alone for the rest of his days, but there was a special sort of magic about her that had changed him, brought him back to how he used to be, and whatever happened between them he would always be grateful to her for that.

But before Saturday there was a busy week at the practice to be got through, with personal feelings put to one side and health care a priority. Valerie Seddon, the patient who'd had the heart attack at the surgery, was still in Coronary Care but improving, and Dave Lorimer was home with a shaven head and brighter hopes for the future. Both satisfactory outcomes of serious situations.

But it wasn't like that for everyone. An elderly patient who had been unwell for some time had been told that blood tests had shown she had an iron deficiency. Assuming that a course of iron tablets would solve the problem, she'd been dismayed to be told that it could be a sign of cancer, and that she would have to go for tests.

Her problem was the kind that cropped up all the time as lots of things did, but not so with Coralie Stephens, who had been rushed into hospital with what had appeared to be a stroke and had turned out to be nothing of the kind.

Her husband, a farmer, had been worried about her for some time as she'd suddenly gone deaf and spent most of her days in bed, feeling ill.

Matthew had visited her a few times and hadn't been happy that a hospital appointment she'd been given had taken so long. But before it had arrived, she had suffered what her husband had thought a stroke and he'd taken her straight to hospital.

Tests had shown that the sudden paralysis was not a stroke. They'd discovered fluid in her ears and the doctors attending her had been baffled by her condition until one of them had suggested that she might be suffering from a very rare illness called Wegener's granulomatosis, and that was what it had turned out to be.

When Matthew found out what the diagnosis was he was horrified. Henrietta hadn't even heard of it.

'It's a collection of abnormal cells that develop in the nasal passages, the lungs and the kidneys,' he explained, 'and you can bet it's what has been causing Coralie's deafness. There are all sorts of unpleasant side issues to it. Inflammation of the eyes, skin ulcers, heart problems, kidney failure. The only good thing is that patients usually recover from it. But it can take up to twelve months.'

'Was all this in the hospital's report?' she'd asked.

'No. I haven't got it yet. Her husband has just been in to tell me what's been happening as he knows I've been concerned about her and anxious that she should start some sort of treatment. But it took nature to push the matter in the form of the paralysis that caused him to rush her into hospital.'

'Does he know how they're going to treat her?'

'Yes, and it's not pleasant. Steroids, chemotherapy, even though it's not cancer-related, and immunosupressant drugs, because it's an illness brought about by the body's natural defences attacking its own tissues.'

'Poor woman.'

'Yes, indeed,' he agreed sombrely. 'I've known Coralie and Jim a long time and they're great people. He was in a state when he came in to see me.'

'I'm sure he was.' As they went to face the patients of the day she'd said, 'After hearing about that anything we have to deal with today couldn't possibly be as bad.'

'I wouldn't bank on that,' he remarked dryly.

Saturday came at last and when Henrietta went upstairs in the early evening to get changed it seemed unreal. She saw lots of Matthew at the practice and while they were doing the decorating, but tonight would be different. Just the two of them in an intimate setting. It would be as he'd said before when they'd planned to spend the day together—no practice, no decorating and, for a little while, no children.

Did Matthew see it as a date, she wondered, or just a pleasant evening with a friend? No doubt she would soon find out. He was bringing Kate with him and once she was settled in with the children they would be off to the Goose.

When Henrietta opened the door to him and Kate, with the children on either side of her, Mollie in her nightdress and Keiran in his pyjamas, Matthew smiled at the trio who had captured his heart, and Kate gave a satisfied nod as if to say, So far, so good.

Henrietta had chosen the outfit she liked best out of her wardrobe. A sleeveless, calf-length dress of cream silk, with a tight-fitting, dark green jacket. She'd put her hair up and fastened it with the same gold comb that had held it on the night Matthew had kissed her, hoping that it might turn out to be a good-luck charm.

It being Saturday night, the Goose was busy, and as they were shown to their table with the smiling courtesy shown to a regular guest, Henrietta wondered how many times Matthew had dined there alone.

Too many to count, no doubt, but at least it had been one night of the week when he'd sallied forth from the drab house that wasn't drab any more. The transformation was almost complete and she smiled at the thought.

He was watching her expression from across the table

and said, 'It seems that something pleases you. I hope it's this place.'

'It's very nice,' she told him. 'Much more upmarket than I expected. I can't remember when last I dined in a place like this, but the smile was for something else. I was thinking that your house is almost finished and how attractive it looks.'

'And what brought that thought to mind?'

'Remembering how our lives used to be, and what they're like now. Me in the big city, never knowing what was coming next, always on my guard, and you shutting yourself away once the surgery was closed, giving everything you had to give to your patients because you had no one else to give it to, except Kate. But you did at least come here once each week.'

'What did you do on Saturday nights when you lived in Manchester?'

'Nothing as pleasant as this, I can assure you.'

'So you've no regrets about coming to live here?'

'You know I haven't. Even though you were so grumpy when we first met, I was already hooked on country life. I've never forgotten the home visits we did together during my first days here. Mrs Carradine at Goyt Lodge and the vet's little girl were far from run of the mill.'

'Yes, that was when you picked up on the atmosphere between Roger Martin and myself. I don't blame the vet *or* his wife and daughter for what happened to Joanna, and I've accepted that his son was just indulging in stupid teenage bravado. But how do you think I felt when I saw Joanna lying there? It was such a waste. A terrible, unnecessary waste.

'It was school holidays and she was out walking with the ramblers. The Martin lad was larking about near a big drop up amongst the peaks and when he saw Joanna coming, way in front of the others, he pretended to fall over the edge. But it was a bit too realistic. He lost his footing and went over. Lucky for him he landed in a bush not far from the top that broke his fall.

'When she saw what had happened Joanna reached over and began to pull him up. He was scared stiff and when she had him almost at the top he flung himself upwards while still holding onto her, and as he reached safety the force of his grip pulled her forward and she went hurtling down onto rocks below.

'Somebody rang me at the surgery and I got there at the same time as the ambulance, but it was too late. She was dead. Gone from me without a goodbye. If I could have got my hands on that young idiot I don't know what I might have done. Fortunately for him he'd been rushed to hospital suffering from severe shock.'

Henrietta reached across the table and took his hand in hers. 'No one should have that sort of grief thrust upon them,' she said softly. 'Yet so many people do. But you've come through it, haven't you? You're ready to move on and, whatever you decide to do, I hope that it will make you truly happy.'

She was giving him an opening to say what was in his mind, Matthew thought, yet he had a feeling that she would drop his hand like a hot coal if he told her, as all he was getting from her was a squeeze of the hand and her blessing. And he wanted more than that. Much more.

* * *

There was a dance floor in the centre of the restaurant and when they'd finished eating, Matthew said, 'Do you like dancing?'

She smiled across at him. 'Yes. I love to dance, though I've never had the time to come up with a polished performance.'

'Same here,' he said easily, getting to his feet. 'Shall we see what we can accomplish together?'

We could accomplish lots of things together, she thought as they moved slowly around the floor. Matthew's touch could be the promise of things to come. His nearness the beginning of desire. Closing her eyes, she gave herself up to the moment and he said softly, 'No perfume tonight.'

She shook her head. 'No. I feel it belongs to the past.' She took a deep breath. 'Just as your lovely wife does.'

He was staring at her incredulously. 'I told you the story of what happened to Joanne because it *is* the past. Not because I'm still dwelling on it but because I thought you should know exactly what happened, as I've only mentioned it briefly before, and then I would put it to rest. But it seems that you think I enjoy being maudlin and self-pitying.'

With his hand under her elbow he was walking her back to the table and she thought, So much for a lovely evening. She had angered him. Had known when she'd spoken that it might upset him, yet she'd still said it. Which had to mean that she still had doubts about how far he had come in saying goodbye to his wife.

There was silence in the car as he drove them back to The White House, the silence of anger on his part and regret on hers. Henrietta hoped she would be able to dredge up a serene expression for Kate's benefit.

She spent the rest of the weekend in a state of misery, analysing and dissecting every word they'd said, and kept reaching the dismal conclusion that she must have doubts about Matthew, or she wouldn't have said what she had.

Yet only minutes earlier she'd been going on about how he'd changed. He must be thinking that it was time she made up her mind.

There was no word or sight of Matthew during Sunday, and every time Henrietta picked up the phone to ring him she put it back as if it was burning her fingers. By Monday morning she was so desperate to see him again she found herself counting the minutes.

He was on the phone, talking to Doulgas, the practice manager, when she arrived at the surgery and was frowning when he replaced the receiver.

'Douglas wants to come in during the lunch-hour to show us estimates for the decorating of this place,' he said in a voice that had no warmth in it. 'I'd intended visiting young Daniel then. He's in hospital at the moment, enduring some physiotherapy to try and give him some mobility. The chances are not good and the lad needs all the support he can get, but I suppose I could go this evening.'

'I can deal with Douglas if you like,' she suggested, with a smile that was strained around the edges. 'You know I'm good with colour schemes. I suppose they'll be ready to hang the curtains and fit the carpets at your place any day.'

'Soon,' he said flatly, 'and, yes, you can sort Douglas out when he comes, if you don't mind.' And on that cheerful note he went to deal with his patients.

There was definitely frost in the air, she thought when he'd gone, but at least she was where she could see him. The longing to be held by him, kissed by him, made love to by him was still there. It wasn't ever going to go away, but for now she was going to have to be satisfied with their working relationship.

The headmistress of the children's school rang in the middle of surgery to say that she was sorry to hear from Mollie that she'd been unwell over the weekend, and that some of the other children had been the same to varying degrees. They suspected that it was due to a very strong-smelling varnish that had been used by men decorating a new annex next to the children's classroom.

'The smell was quite pungent,' she explained, 'and after the first coating we asked them not to use it any more. But by then it was giving off some nasty fumes and about a dozen or so of the children have had a reaction to them, including your niece, it would seem.

'We normally have any decorating done during the long summer break,' she went on to say, 'but this new building is needed for the end-of-term play that we are presenting to parents and friends. I understand that Keiran and Mollie's parents are abroad and won't be able to attend, but we would be pleased to see you there if you can manage it, Dr Mason.'

'I'll do my best,' Henrietta promised, 'and with regard

to the children being ill from the fumes you describe, I'm not happy about that. The firm concerned should have checked that kind of thing before using it near children. I suppose it was one of the new miracle fast-drying substances that have a lot of chemicals in them.

'Fortunately Mollie seems to have recovered from its effects and I am presuming that the other children who were also affected are now over it, but it could have ended up a serious matter.'

'Yes, I do know that,' the headmistress said contritely, 'and I can assure you that it will not happen again.'

Matthew had appeared halfway through the phone call and when she'd finished talking to the headmistress he said, 'So it was paint fumes.'

'Yes, it would appear so. As you'll have just heard I have expressed my concern. Do you think the children who were affected should be checked over? Chest or lung X-rays maybe?'

'Yes, I do. One can't be too careful with that kind of thing and Mollie's breathing was a bit shallow at the time. I would get back on to the school and suggest that they tell the parents of those children that were affected to take them to A and E to be checked over. Better be safe than sorry.'

"I'll have to take Mollie this evening when I've finished here.'

'If you want some moral support, I'll come with you.'

'Are you sure? I know I'm not exactly your favourite person at the moment.'

'Don't make something out of nothing, Henrietta, and, yes, I am sure. I never say anything I don't mean. We can

ABIGAIL GORDON   151

finish early here and pick the children up straight from the school bus. If the headmistress had come up with this information a bit sooner, we could have taken Mollie to hospital yesterday.'

'I suppose she would have if it hadn't been the weekend, but they'll only have discovered how many children were affected when school started this morning. They are putting on an end-of-term play and I've been invited to be there to represent Pamela and Charles.'

'When is it?'

'Next week. The last day of July and end of the school year.'

'You'll enjoy that, won't you?'

'Er…yes, I will, but it will feel odd on my own. I wish their parents could be here for them on that sort of occasion.'

'If you want my opinion, which I know you don't, I think they should be there for them all the time. They are missing precious months with Mollie and Keiran that won't come again. What would they have done if you hadn't been available?'

'Boarding school.'

He tutted angrily and Henrietta read his mind. He was thinking that he had been denied children because the only woman he'd ever wanted to give them to him had been killed. While others left their children for months on end and didn't bat an eyelid.

'Pamela and Charles do love the children,' she told him chidingly, 'but they may have different ideas about bringing them up to what we have. Anyway, they'll be home sooner than they planned. I won't be needed any more then as they'll be closing the house when they take the children back with them.'

'You may not be needed there any more, but I'll still want you with me at the surgery.'

'Yes, maybe until John Lomas comes back. Then it will be a case of getting used to city life again.'

'I thought you liked it here,' he said, aghast to think that he might be driving her back to where she'd come from with his indifference.

'I do. I love it, but things change, don't they?'

'Yes, they do,' he agreed heavily, and left it at that.

The only person who seemed to be enjoying the visit to the emergency section of the nearest hospital was Keiran—mainly because he wasn't the patient and also because he was immediately fascinated by the bustling health-care set-up.

Matthew hadn't had much to say since their conversation about different people's ideas of bringing up children. Mollie was tearful at the thought of what lay ahead, in spite of being held close and reassured that there was nothing to be afraid of. And Henrietta was wondering what she was going to say to Pamela if her child had been affected by the paint fumes in any way other than a minor upset.

'Hi, Matthew,' a doctor in A and E said with a raising of the eyebrows and a glance in her direction. 'This your family?'

He shook his head. 'No. They're the children of friends. How's your gang?' Turning to Henrietta, he said, 'Jason and I were at college together. He's got twin girls and an older boy.' He turned to his friend. 'This is Dr Henrietta

Mason, the other doctor in my practice and stand-in mother at the moment.'

Henrietta held back a groan. Why were they always being paired off by those who knew little about them? Especially when the two of them seemed to be drifting apart.

For the first time in her life she had found a man that she could love and cherish with all her being, and if he didn't want her she would never turn to anyone else. So if you want Matthew Cazalet, go out and get him, the voice of reason said. But it wasn't that easy when one was competing with a memory.

Since they'd arrived at A and E Matthew's moroseness of earlier had disappeared and he was teasing Mollie gently while X-rays were being done. When they were given the all-clear he swooped her up in his arms to carry her out to the car and she cuddled against him, happy that it was all over.

'Do you want to come in and eat with us?' Henrietta asked uncomfortably when they eventually pulled up in the drive outside The White House. 'Kate always leaves stacks of food.'

He shook his head, the coolness back once more. 'No, thanks. She'll have made a meal for us at my place.'

Henrietta nodded, then on impulse stepped up to him and hugged him. 'Thank you being there for us once again,' she said softly, and, looking into his surprised dark gaze, she cupped his face in her hands and kissed him gently on the mouth.

'Very nice,' he said in the same cool tone. 'But make up your mind, Henrietta.' He moved away from her and said,

'Take care, and don't forget to make sure that all is secure before it goes dark.'

She nodded. So much for seduction. But was a man like Matthew going to recognise a fleeting kiss as that?

When the children were tucked up for the night and she was about to go downstairs, Keiran said, 'You'll have to marry Uncle Matthew now.'

'Why will I have to do that?'

'We saw you kiss him, didn't we, Mollie?'

Almost asleep after the day's events, his sister mumbled, 'Yes, we did, Aunt Henny. Shall I start collecting rose petals?'

'Not just yet. There's no rush. People who are just friends kiss each other too, you know,' she told them, trying to keep a straight face. 'Now, sleep well.'

Alone in the sitting room with the summer night closing in around her, Henrietta was deep in thought. She'd made the first move towards letting Matthew see how she felt, but it hadn't been easy and a swift peck on the lips wasn't going to get her far.

She would have her hair cut, she decided. Instead of the long swathe of it down her back. She would have a shorter, more feminine style that took the attention off her height.

And clothes. Once the children were on the long summer holiday from school they would have a day in the city centre and do some intensive shopping, she was deciding when there was the sound of the door to the patio opening and a strange voice called, 'Anybody there?'

When she hurried to investigate there was an unkempt, bearded man framed in the doorway, weather-beaten, and dressed in clothes that had seen much wear and tear. Immediately Matthew's warnings about security came to mind.

'Where's the missus?' he asked as Henrietta observed him unsmilingly. 'She usually sorts me out some grub.'

It was almost dark and she switched on the kitchen lights quickly. 'Who are you?' she asked, trying to sound cool with the thought of the children sleeping up above and this fellow only a few feet away.

'Mark McIvor is the name. I sleep rough. I'm here because the lady of the house gives me food when I'm passing this way. Good food it is, too, and while I'm in the village the doctor down at the practice checks me over.'

Henrietta relaxed slightly. 'You mean Dr Cazalet?'

'Aye, I do.'

'What does my sister usually give you?'

'Milk, bread, meat, cake if there's any going spare, and anything else that's surplus. Where is she?'

Not entirely convinced by what he was saying, there was no way that she was going to let him see that Pamela and Charles weren't around, so she said, 'They've just gone down to the village and will be back any moment. I'll see what I can find you.'

With a speed that came from apprehension she filled a plastic bag with food and handed it to him.

He touched his tattered hat. 'Thank you kindly, miss.' As he turned to go he said, 'Will it be all right if I bed down for the night at the other side of the bottom hedge? I won't make a mess.'

'Yes, I suppose so,' she told him doubtfully, and the moment he'd gone she phoned Matthew.

'Henrietta,' he said flatly.

'There's been a man at the patio door,' she said, trying to sound calm.

'I take it that the door was locked?'

'Er, no,' she said awkwardly.

'Are you insane?' he bellowed. 'It's almost dark. Where is he now?'

'Gone to sleep at the bottom of the garden. He was dirty and weatherbeaten and said that every time he passes this way Pamela gives him some food, which sounded reasonable enough, but I want to be sure he won't harm us.'

'I don't believe I'm hearing this.'

She could hardly tell him that she'd forgotten to lock the door because she'd been daydreaming about him. But she needed to know if it was true when the man had said that Matthew knew him.

'He says that he—'

'I'm not interested in what he says,' he interrupted. 'I'm on my way.' And the line went dead.

She hadn't wanted him to come over. All she'd needed was to know if he knew this Mark McIvor, but he hadn't given her time to ask.

All right, she knew she should have locked the door, and this was going to be another black mark against her. But did Matthew have to be so scathing about it?

The homeless man's appearance was the last thing she'd been expecting. It was surprising that Pamela hadn't warned her about his visits. She would have been less taken aback then.

Remembering how Matthew had been there for them at the hospital earlier, it was as if he was doing everything right and she was doing everything wrong.

CHAPTER NINE

AS HE drove the short distance to The White House, Matthew's expression was sombre. He had let himself fall in love with Henrietta. Had come out from behind the protective shield that he'd lived behind since losing Joanna, and now was as vulnerable as any other man whose heart had been captured by a woman.

She was always in his thoughts. He was aware of how alone she was, in spite of having her sister and her family in her life, and was constantly wanting to be near her. Aching to make love to her. All feelings that had been long dead until she'd appeared on the scene.

Was this new love, this crazy passion he'd developed for Henrietta, going to turn him into some sort of a puppet dancing on a string? he wondered. He may have been miserable before, but at least he'd been able to sleep at night.

When he arrived, the windows were blazing with light and dominating the landscape in the summer dusk. All appeared to be calm, but it wasn't what was going on from the outside that mattered. He wanted to know what was going on inside, that Henrietta and the children were safe.

'Where is this man now?' he asked the moment she opened the door.

'There's smoke coming from the bottom of the garden,' she told him, 'so I imagine he's cooking himself a meal from the food I gave him. He had an old frypan with him.'

'Is he? We'll see about that. I'm not having him hanging about round here while you and the children are on your own,' he said tightly.

'He says he knows you.'

About to go charging down the garden, Matthew stopped in his tracks.

'He knows *me*?'

'Yes. He said his name is Mark McIvor.'

'Ah! Of course! Old Mark always appears in these parts in the late summer. If you'd said he'd told you who he was, I wouldn't have got so steamed up.'

'I would have done if you'd given me time, but you put the phone down and set off for here as if I'm some sort of witless creature who can't cope.'

'The day will never dawn when I think that,' he said with a tight smile. 'So why did you phone me, then? Why do that if you didn't want me to come? Were you expecting me to just go to bed after what you'd told me?'

'I admit that I was a bit apprehensive when he first appeared,' she said, not to be placated. 'But it was mainly on the children's behalf. I've been in situations much worse than that when I worked in Manchester.'

'There is no need to be so uppity,' he pointed out. 'If I'd known the full circumstances, I wouldn't have interfered. Mark McIvor does appear around these parts about this time every year and he's quite harmless, wouldn't hurt a fly. I had no idea that he called here on his travels, otherwise it might have occurred to me to mention it. But top marks to your sister for helping the homeless.'

'It's good to know that one of us has your approval,' she told him stiffly, 'though it's been a long time coming, as far as Pamela is concerned.'

'So you don't want me to be concerned about your welfare?' he questioned, without taking her up on the comment about her sister.

Of course she did, Henrietta thought miserably. She wanted them to look after each other, wrapped around with love. She wanted to give him the babies he longed for, but did he see her in that role? Friend, colleague, yes, but not someone to give his bruised heart to.

'I'll go and have a word with Mark,' he said levelly, 'and fix up for him to come to my place for a bath and a check-up, and then I'll go.'

Misery washed over her as he went out through the patio door and strode off to where spirals of smoke were rising at the other side of the bottom hedge.

When he came back Matthew avoided the house and went straight to his car, and as she watched from the window Henrietta couldn't believe how she'd thrown his concern back in his face. He *had* been a bit over the top, but she had been at fault for not locking up after his reminder.

She'd told herself when she'd phoned him that it was just to ask if he knew the man, to put her mind at rest, but she admitted that underneath she'd hoped he would come. And, of course, he had, at top speed, but he'd brought annoyance with him, and she'd resented it and been snappy with him.

I wish I'd never come to this place, she thought dismally. Everyone here knows each other, except me. I came to take care of the children and found the man of my dreams. Yet where has it got me? After treasuring every moment we spend together, I've just spoilt it with a few heated words.

He'd just behaved like a prize fusspot, Matthew thought as he drove home. Ranting and raving like a Victorian father. Henrietta was right. She was able to look after herself. But the trouble was he was in love with her, and with love came caring.

Before she'd come into his life he'd had only Kate and himself to think about, but when he committed himself to something he didn't do it by halves, and that applied to falling in love. Whether he wanted it or not, he was back in the real world and not sure how much he was enjoying being there.

Matthew was late arriving at the practice the next morning, which was most unusual, and as the minutes ticked by and there was no message Henrietta began to feel uneasy. It was her turn to be anxious, she thought wryly. Maybe Matthew was out to teach her a lesson and it didn't matter if he was, just as long as he was all right.

She had already started seeing her patients when she heard his voice in Reception and her spirits lifted. In a few moments she would see him and come alive, in spite of the previous night's disagreement.

But he didn't open her door to say good morning. His footsteps went past and straight into his own room and the brightness that his arrival had brought was dimmed.

Meriel Martin, the vet's wife, was one of those waiting to see her. Henrietta hadn't met her before as she'd been away looking after a sick relative on the day that she and Matthew had made a home visit to their small daughter.

She was a plump, motherly-looking woman and Henrietta immediately thought how dreadful it must have been, and most likely still was, to know that one's child had been responsible for someone's death.

'The top of my foot started to swell over the weekend,' Meriel explained, 'and even though I bathed it with witch hazel, which I swear by for that kind of thing, it has had no effect. Now it's extremely painful. I had a similar swelling on my hand a couple of months ago and antibiotics cleared it more or less. But there is still some inflammation there that seems to come and go.'

Her foot was bright red and very shiny and as Henrietta examined it she asked, 'Have you ever had cellulitis?'

'Yes,' was the reply, 'but it was many years ago.'

'I'm going to have your blood levels tested for glucose and uric acid,' she told her. 'Cellulitis, gout and erysipelas are all diseases connected with inflammation of the body tissues, and this kind of thing can also be caused by diabetes. So we need to be sure where it's coming from. In the meantime, I'm going to prescribe an antibiotic called flucloxacillin, which should clear up the infection.

'If you'd like to pop along to one of the nurses, she'll do

the blood tests. Phone towards the end of the week to see if we've got the results, and then I'll need to see you again.'

As she got to her feet Meriel said hesitantly, 'How is Dr Cazalet these days?'

'In what way?'

'Er…is he any happier. Or more relenting? I'm sure he will have told you what happened.'

'Yes, he has,' Henrietta said softly, 'and I think the answer to both your questions is yes. But you should ask him yourself, shouldn't you? It isn't really for me to say.'

'Our boy has been abroad ever since it happened,' Meriel explained, her pleasant face crumpling, 'but he can't stay there for ever. We miss him terribly. But though I'm longing to have him back with us, I'm dreading it, too. We don't want to cause Matthew any more pain.'

'I'm sure you don't. Why not just let it happen and take each day as it comes? It will be a difficult time for all of you, but I'm sure that Matthew won't want to make it any more distressing for your family.'

The other woman nodded. 'I hope you're right, Dr Mason. We all need some kind of closure.'

When she'd gone Henrietta sat back and thought about what the vet's wife had said. She was right. They did need closure and she hoped that Matthew would see it that way. He was a kind and loving man who had suffered great pain, and was now throwing off its bonds, ready for a new beginning.

It was lunchtime before they came face to face and he said, as if nothing was amiss, 'I'm sorry I didn't get the chance to phone in to say I would be late. It was a bit hectic at my place first thing. McIvor came for a bath and a check-up, which all took time, and then there was the cleaning up afterwards.'

'Did you have time for any breakfast?'

'No. I didn't, and who's fussing now?'

'I am. I'm so sorry about last night, Matthew. I was a pain and an unreasonable one at that. Can I take you for a nice lunch somewhere between house calls and the late surgery to make up for it?'

'I doubt we'll have time,' he said, 'especially if we had to wait to be served. Why don't we pick up something from the village bakery and drive up on to the tops for half an hour?'

'Yes,' she said immediately, relieved to be back on their usual footing. 'I'll go to the bakery at the beginning of the lunch-hour, and if you bring your car round and wait outside while I'm served, we can make a quick getaway.'

When lunchtime came and she'd bought the food, he drove to the top of the hill road where bracken, gorse and ripening windberries grew on the bleak terrain.

There was silence between them in the car as they ate the food and washed it down with fruit juice, but once they'd finished Henrietta turned to him and said, 'I have something to tell you.'

Matthew needed to know that the vet's son would soon be home, and it might be better that he found out from her now rather than later from Kate or one of the villagers. Being the messenger with that sort of news wouldn't endear her to him, but at least he would have heard it in private.

He was winding down the car window, letting in air that was fresh and fumeless, and she saw him tense. Did he already know? she thought uneasily. And wasn't going to thank her for a second telling of it?

Henrietta is going to leave the practice, he was thinking. She's weary of working with a control freak. Last night must have been one step too far. She'd said she was sorry for being snappy, but it didn't mean that she was going to put up with his interfering any more.

She had begun to speak in a low voice and he had to drag his thoughts back from where they'd wandered to. As he tuned in to what she was saying he picked up on, 'She said that her son is coming back to the village to live.'

He stared at her blankly. 'Who did?'

'Meriel Martin. The vet's wife. She came to consult me this morning with an infected foot. and told me that they can't bear to be away from their son any longer, so he's coming home and she's hoping that...'

'I'll be amenable.'

'Yes, something like that.'

'I suppose you might have had worse things to tell me, though not much. For instance, you could have been going to tell me that you're leaving the practice.'

'I'd only do that if you didn't need me any more!' she exclaimed. She loved the job almost as much as she loved the man.

'It was just a thought that I picked up from your expression.'

'If I looked solemn it was because of what I had to tell you, but I thought the news might be less painful coming from an outsider.'

'Outsider! Is that what you see yourself as?'

'Yes, sort of, but it isn't a problem. Pamela and her family are part of the local fraternity, whatever their life-style. Kate is the very personification of all that is best in village life, and you…'

Her voice trailed away. If she started telling him what she thought of him she would give herself away, and there was nothing more mortifying than the person one was in love with becoming aware of it when they didn't have the same feelings.

'Yes, me. What am I?' he asked dryly.

'You're the focal point of the place. So many depend on you. The way you run the practice is so stressless and caring I couldn't believe it when I first came here after the hustle and bustle of my last job.'

'I know I didn't think that during those first few days. You were prickly as a hedgehog, but the feeling didn't last and I soon got to know the real you.'

No mention of any attraction, he noticed. Just the good old GP looking after his patients.

He checked the time. 'We'd better be getting back, Henrietta, or they'll be sending out a search party, and if it gets around that we've been alone up here with not a soul in sight, your reputation will be tarnished for ever.'

For the rest of the week Henrietta debated whether to ask Matthew to go to the school play with her. She knew how much he enjoyed being with the children, but didn't want him to think she was pushing it after their clash of wills on the night that Mark McIvor appeared.

They were back on good terms now, though only as the

friendly colleagues they'd been before. But she wasn't giving up on him. She wanted Matthew. Wanted him in her life, her bed, her every waking moment, and the school play could be a move in the right direction.

It was to take place on the Wednesday of the following week and after that Mollie and Keiran would be at home for the long summer break and she was concerned about what they were going to do while she was working.

Maybe Kate would keep an eye on them for part of the day, or she could ask Matthew for fewer hours or take leave. But she hadn't been at the practice long enough to have earned much vacation time.

Her sister might be good at organising, but she hadn't made provision for that, she thought. The summer holidays were a long time for children not to be happily occupied in a safe environment.

They had come home from school with two tickets for the play, so she had a good excuse for asking Matthew if he wanted to go with them, and when she mentioned it he said, 'I thought you'd never ask.'

'I've been hesitating because I thought you might feel you'd spent enough of your free time out of working hours with us.'

He frowned. 'What about *your* free time, which you've given so generously while we've been decorating my house?'

'That was my pleasure,' she said, smiling across at him.

'And you think the giving of *my* time wasn't?'

'I don't know, do I?'

'Well, you should. So what time does this play start and what is it?'

'*Wind In The Willows*. The children are trees, so we might have some aching arms afterwards. We'll need to leave the village about sixish to give them time to get changed and for us to be settled in our seats, as it starts at seven.

'Mollie and Keiran will be coming home as usual in the afternoon and Kate will be making us a meal as she normally does, so why don't we all eat together. It would be less hassle for her.'

'Why not?' he agreed with a lift to his voice. To be sitting close to Henrietta for a couple of hours during the play would be blissful, and sharing a meal with her and the children before that would be an added pleasure.

'We'll have to sort something about the school holidays, won't we?' he said later that day. 'Have you had any thoughts about how you're going to cope with the job and the children? You can have time off if you want. Kate has said that she'll help out in any way she can if you want her to, and I can be flexible at the surgery if need be.'

'You're always one step ahead of me, aren't you?' she said, as tears pricked at his thoughtfulness.

'Do you think so? I would have thought lagging behind described my function in your life.'

'And whose fault is that?' she asked, as she made her way to where one of the practice nurses was waiting for them to start the antenatal clinic.

Meriel Martin's blood tests were back and when she came in for the results Henrietta had to tell her that the pathology department were asking for another test, this time after fasting. The vet's wife was immediately anxious and wanted to know why.

'It's most likely because something has shown up borderline and they want a definite diagnosis,' she told her. 'Try not to get agitated about it. We'll know soon enough what has caused the inflammation in your foot. At the moment the antibiotics are doing a great job. I see that the swelling has almost gone. But we need to know why it happened, and once we know that we can treat the cause.'

She was hoping there would no more mention of matters that had occurred before she'd come to live in the village, and to her relief this time there wasn't. Reception would give Meriel an early morning appointment after she'd fasted from the night before, and it would be wait-and-see time again. All neatly arranged, but it didn't stop Henrietta from wondering what would happen when the son came home.

'I'm looking forward to the children's stage debut,' Matthew said on Wednesday morning.

'Yes, so am I,' she told him, and thought that a school play, seated on hard chairs that made a scraping noise when moved, next to a cloakroom smelling of sweaty trainers, wasn't exactly moonlight and roses, but if Matthew was as attracted to her as she was to him, none of that would matter.

At the moment she didn't know what was going on in his mind, but one thing she did know was that some unseen force was pulling her towards him. Whether it was having the same effect on him she had yet to find out. Sometimes the pull was so strong she felt that he must be aware of it.

But knowing him, if he had something to say he would have said it by now. Maybe he was around so much because he was enjoying spending time with Mollie and Keiran and she was the way to them, she thought sombrely.

Having seen him with the kids, she thought that he really should have a family of his own. But he'd probably worked that out for himself and didn't need her to point the way.

As they all sat around the dining table at The White House that evening, Matthew, Henrietta, Kate and the children, he said whimsically, 'I could take to family life like a duck to water.'

It was all pretence, of course. The only one present who was his family was Kate. The children belonged to someone else and as for Henrietta she seemed determined to keep him guessing.

Seated across the table from him, her glance was on Kate and she saw that his aunt's eyes were moist, but her voice was brisk enough as she said, 'So do something about it, Matthew.'

'I intend to,' he said smoothly, and carried on eating.

He was still dressed in the dark suit that he'd worn to the practice, having had no time to go home to change, but Henrietta had dashed upstairs the moment they'd arrived at the house and changed her working clothes for a long beige tiered skirt and a pale apricot top that made her skin glow and brought out the lights in her hair.

There was nothing she could do to make herself small and cuddly, she'd decided, but she did have some physical assets and may as well use them. If she was going to have

Matthew to herself while they watched the play, she was going to make the most of it.

It hadn't gone unnoticed and Matthew had moved to stand by the window, gazing out over the gardens when she appeared. Otherwise he wouldn't have been able to resist taking her in his arms and kissing her until she begged for mercy. But Kate had been buzzing in and out of the kitchen and the children had been toing and froing and he hadn't wanted to put on a show for them.

There wasn't time to linger over the meal and soon they were on their way to the school with the children hyped up in the back seat at the thought of the night ahead, and the two adults so aware of each other it was like a fast fire burning.

Henrietta's gaze was on Matthew's hands. Capable, strong, with well kept nails, they were gentle with those whose needs brought them to him. They would be safe hands to be loved by, she thought, and she found herself hungering for his touch.

As if aware of her thoughts, he took his glance off the road for a second and with a raised eyebrow asked, 'What? What are you looking at?'

'Your hands.'

'My hands!' Amusement glinted in the dark eyes looking into hers. 'Why? Were you checking to see if my nails are clean before I meet the headmistress?'

'No. Nothing like that.'

'What, then? Are you going to tell me?'

'Not at this moment.'

The school had appeared on the skyline and the children were getting more excited by the minute. The explanation that Matthew was waiting for would have to wait, but as he parked the car he said in a low voice, 'You haven't got away with it, you know. I will still want to know what is so fascinating about my hands.'

She pretended not to hear and ushered Mollie and Keiran towards the main entrance. As the children made a beeline for a teacher who was directing operations, the two doctors waved goodbye and joined the crush of parents and friends trying to find a seat.

The play was rather wordy with quite a degree of talent amongst some of the older pupils, but it was on two small trees that Henrietta and Matthew had their eyes fixed, and she took some photos to send to Pamela and Charles.

After the play was over refreshments were served in the school canteen, with tea and biscuits for the adults and fruit juice for the children. As Mollie and Keiran chattered excitedly beside them, Matthew said to Henrietta in a low voice, 'I don't believe it. We haven't been mistaken for their parents.'

She smiled. 'Do you wish you were?'

His gaze had darkened. 'There are some parts of the arrangement that would suit me very well, but with regard to children, I would prefer to start from scratch, as Mollie and Keiran, delightful though they are, belong to someone else.'

He watched the colour rise in her cheeks, waiting for a response, but it wasn't forthcoming. Henrietta was thinking achingly that she didn't want to have to listen to hidden meanings. She was in love with Matthew and wanted straight talk from him if he had anything to say, so she gave him a cool smile and changed the subject.

'I think we need to be making tracks,' she said in a tone that matched the smile. 'It's been a long day for the children, though they don't have to get up early for school tomorrow, thank goodness. I spoke to Kate this morning and she has agreed to keep an eye on them in the mornings, and if you'll agree to me finishing after I've done the house calls, the time they would normally be at school will be covered.'

'Yes, of course. Take the afternoons off,' he said easily, as if he hadn't just been sidetracked.

As they were going to the car, which was parked near the school gates Keiran was in front, dribbling a ball that he'd found somewhere, and Mollie was walking between the two doctors, holding their hands. Without warning, a car with luggage piled on the roof came careerning through the gates at speed.

The driver was slumped over the wheel and Keiran was standing transfixed in its path, not knowing where to run as it was zigzagging from side to side. As Henrietta plunged forward, Matthew was faster and with the car almost on him pushed the terrified child out of its path. But there was no time to save himself. The out-of-control vehicle hit him and then veered sideways into a car parked nearby and came to a standstill.

Mollie was crying and Keiran standing mutely beside his sister as Henrietta ran towards Matthew, lying on the tarmac of the car park.

'Stay there, children,' she cried over her shoulder. 'Don't move!' And then she was on her knees beside him. He was on his back, unconscious, with blood running down his face and spreading out from underneath his head, but he was breathing, she thought thankfully, and after checking his airway she reached for her phone and dialled the emergency services.

'Two ambulances needed, fast,' she said when the call was answered. 'A double accident at Moncreith Junior School. One person unconscious, and the other collapsed and crashed his car. He appears to be moving, but you must hurry.'

While she'd been phoning, people had been running from the school building, having heard the noise of the runaway car crashing into the other vehicle.

A teacher had taken charge of Mollie and Keiran and some of the fathers who'd been at the play were trying to open the doors of the car to get the driver out. Another teacher, who said she was trained in first aid, went to help while Henrietta stayed with Matthew.

At that moment there was a loud cry and a mother with three young children at her heels came running towards them. 'That's our car!' she was crying. 'What's happened?'

Henrietta was barely aware of what was going on around her. Matthew was hurt. He'd risked his life for Keiran and taken the brunt of the impact himself. Please, God, don't let him die, she was saying silently over and over as she examined him for further injuries. I love you so much, Matthew. Don't leave me. But he didn't hear her. He was somewhere else in the dark realms of unconsciousness.

CHAPTER TEN

THE headmistress was hovering over her. 'What happened, Dr Mason?' she asked anxiously.

'The car was out of control,' she said tightly. 'The driver was slumped over the wheel and it was heading straight for Keiran. Dr Cazalet pulled him to safety but didn't have time to get out of the way himself. I've asked for two ambulances and they should be here any moment.'

Her glance was on Matthew's left arm. She suspected a fracture from the appearance of it and thought grimly that along with the head injury it was enough to be going on with.

When she looked up the children were beside her with the teacher, and Mollie asked tearfully, 'Is Uncle Matthew going to die, Aunt Henny.'

'Not if I can help it, Mollie,' she said firmly. She turned to the teacher. 'Dr Cazalet's aunt is his nearest relative. Could you ring her for me so that she can meet us at the hospital?'

'Yes, of course,' she said immediately, and followed it with, 'What are you going to do with the children?'

'Take them with me until I can sort something out. I've no one to leave them with.'

She checked Matthew's pulse and heartbeat again. Both were irregular and she wished the ambulance would hurry. He looked so defenceless lying there that she wanted to weep, but it was a time for action, not tears.

'What about the other man?' she asked the teacher. 'How's he doing?'

'He's conscious and I heard someone say something about him being a diabetic who had forgotten to take his medication, which caused him to pass out at the wheel. He's a father at the school.'

At that moment Matthew gave a sighing sort of groan and opened his eyes. 'Henrietta,' he croaked. 'My head hurts.'

'Yes, I know, ' she said gently, relief at having him back in her world making her legs feel weak. 'Lie still until the ambulance gets here. You fell backwards and cracked your head on the tarmac. Also I think you might have a fracture of your left arm.'

He had closed his eyes but was still conscious. 'Is Keiran all right?'

'Yes. He's not having much to say, but he's fine—not a scratch on him. I wish I could say the same for you.'

The two ambulances that she'd asked for pulled onto the car park and as a couple of paramedics came hurrying over, a second pair were heading for the injured car driver, who was leaning weakly against the side of his car, with his wife hovering anxiously.

Henrietta explained that she was a doctor and that Matthew's injuries were due to him being hit by the other man's car.

'Do you suspect a skull fracture?' one of them asked.

'It is possible so, please, handle him carefully. I will be following by car with the two children.'

'No,' said Matthew as he was lifted onto a stretcher and transferred to the ambulance. 'Henrietta, go home and put the children to bed. I'll be fine.'

'Oh, yes?' she said gently. 'Do you honestly think I'm going to leave you in this state? The children and I will be right behind you all the way to A and E. And I imagine that Kate won't be long after us.'

As they took Matthew to X-Ray at the hospital Henrietta walked beside the trolley, holding his hand, and the children were trailing behind. When he was finally wheeled back to a cubicle in A and E, Kate had arrived in their absence and was waiting ashen-faced for their return.

'They've been telling me what you did, lad,' she said as tears rolled down her plump cheeks. 'Don't die on me, Matthew. I want to see some young ones of yours before it's my turn to go.'

'No need to fret, Kate,' he said, managing a smile. 'I'm still going to be around to plague you.'

The doctor was approaching and as he came through the curtains of the cubicle with the X-ray plates in his hand and saw them all gathered there, he said, 'Just one of you, if you don't mind.'

As Henrietta made to leave with Mollie and Keiran, Kate said, 'You stay, Henrietta. It's what he'll want.'

She flashed her a grateful smile. 'Thanks, Kate.'

The results could have been worse. The elbow *was* fractured, but the head injuries did not include any serious damage to the skull. There was no internal bleeding or bone fragmentation. But there were deep cuts on the back of Matthew's head that would need stitching, and the arm would have to be put in a cast.

'In view of the period of unconsciousness after the car hit you and the blow to your head, we will be keeping you in for observation for a few days,' the doctor told Matthew. 'And if you're as much on the go as we doctors are in here, I would take advantage of the rest.'

He didn't want a rest, Matthew thought grimly. He wanted to be back at the practice with Henrietta and, with that thought in mind, how was she going to manage with him in this place, and the children on school holidays? Yet he was no fool. What this doctor was saying made sense. He'd just have to grin and bear it.

He nodded. 'OK, you're in charge.' Turning to Henrietta, whose thoughts couldn't have been more different, he said, 'Now, will you please go home, Henrietta, and take Kate with you? Tomorrow we'll discuss how we're going to manage at the practice and still take care of the children.'

She smiled. The terror of losing him was abating. What did a few days matter in a lifetime. If she had to, she would take the children to the practice with her. They could take some games and the receptionists would keep an eye on them.

She stroked his blood-streaked face gently and kissed him on the cheek as she was about to leave him, and as she looked down at him her eyes were soft with tenderness

He gave a twisted smile. 'I know what this is for. You're grateful that I saved Keiran, but it's not your gratitude I want, Henrietta.'

A nurse had appeared and was announcing, 'We're ready to take you to have your head injury seen to and your arm set, Dr Cazalet.' To Henrietta she said, 'You can see him any time tomorrow.'

'Yes, I know,' she said softly. Looking at Matthew, she said, 'Maybe then we can take up where we've left off.'

On the way home Kate said, 'So what are we going to do without him, Henrietta? There's the practice and the children to see to. If you can deal with the patients, I'll look after Mollie and Keiran until you come home. I do that already when they come home from school, so it will be just a bit longer, and it's only for a few days.'

'You are a gem, Kate,' Henrietta told her, adding with a catch in her voice, 'We could have lost him today.'

'Was it my fault, Aunt Henny?' Keiran asked anxiously from the back seat.

'No, it wasn't, my darling,' she assured him. 'It was an accident, and the man in the car didn't mean it to happen.'

They had dropped Kate off at her cottage, and now, with the children fast asleep up above, Henrietta was alone with her thoughts. Out of near tragedy had come the future. Matthew was going to be all right, she thought gratefully. She'd seen some traffic accidents in her time and not everyone came out of them alive. She could so easily have been in the same position as he'd been in when he'd lost Joanna. The one she loved taken from her in an instant.

Tomorrow she was going to tell him how she felt, and

if he didn't return her feelings she would get up, dust herself down, and what? She didn't know.

Henrietta rang the hospital at six o'clock the next morning and was told that Matthew had passed a comfortable night. She doubted it. The phrase was part of hospital jargon. He would be in pain from the fractured arm and would have a very sore head, but it meant that he was stable, that no other problems from the accident had arisen. As she replaced the receiver she knew she was going to be counting every minute until she saw him again.

But before that there were patients to be seen. Practice matters to sort out. Home visits to do. She knew that Matthew wouldn't want her to neglect any of those things.

She managed to call at The White House for ten minutes during the lunch-hour and all was well there with Kate in charge.

'Would it be all right with you if I took the children to see him this afternoon?' Kate asked. 'It will mean us going on the bus, but they might enjoy the novelty of it.'

'Yes, of course,' Henrietta said immediately. 'Matthew will love that.' She went on her way, wishing she could go with them. The earliest she would be able to manage would be after the late surgery. Kate had offered to give the children their evening meal so she would be able to visit Matthew then with an easy mind.

When it came to herself it was another matter She wasn't easy in her mind at all. She might end up a prize fool and, instead of Matthew, have mortification as a bed-fellow for the rest of her life, but she had to know.

* * *

He was up, needless to say, when she got there, sitting in small garden at the end of the ward and looking the worse for wear as he gazed into space. They'd cut his hair away at the back for the stitches. The fractured elbow was resting on the arm of the seat, bulky with the cast, and Henrietta could imagine just how hampered he was going to be with it.

It had been great to see Kate and the children this afternoon, he was telling himself, but it was Henrietta that he was longing to see. When she showed up he was going to clarify a few things. He was going to find out if she was on the defensive all the time because she didn't return his feelings or if it was because she felt that he hadn't really let Joanna go enough to be happy with someone else. Whatever it was, he had to know if she cared. He'd told her that it wasn't gratitude he wanted from her and given the opportunity he was going to tell he what he *did* want from her.

When he looked up she was standing there. She flashed him a tired smile and sat down beside him, still dressed in her working clothes, a black suit with a white silk top and sheer stockings on her long, shapely legs.

'How are you?' she asked gently.

'Better for seeing you,' he replied. 'What sort of a day have you had?'

'All right. Busy, of course. It's what sort of day you've had that matters.'

'My day has been long and thought-provoking.'

'Has it? Mine's been a bit like that, too. I've got something to say to you, Matthew.'

She saw him tense. 'Let's have it, then.'

'Will you marry me?'

He stared at her. 'Are you serious?'

'Yes, very.'

'Oh, Henrietta. I've wanted to ask you the very same question for weeks. But always at the back of my mind was the thought that you might think I was asking you to step into Joanna's shoes.'

She shook her head. 'If that was the only thing making you have second thoughts, you need have no concerns. If I married you the only shoes I would be stepping into would be my own. I would always respect your love for her, but our marriage would have to be mine and yours alone.'

'It was a move in the right direction when you came to live in the village and brought me out of the doldrums,' he said in a voice thick with emotion, and reached out for her with his good arm. 'Of course I'll marry you, my beautiful Henrietta, and as we've got a lot of kisses to catch up on, I suggest we start now.' And they did, unaware that a couple of smiling nurses were watching them from the ward window.

'How soon can we arrange the wedding?' Matthew asked when they came down to earth for a moment. 'I can't wait to make you my wife.'

'How about a harvest wedding? It's not far off, but we could do it,' she suggested. 'Pamela, Charles and the kids will have gone by then, but they'd be able to come back.'

'A harvest wedding would be lovely,' he agreed, smiling at his bride-to-be.

'Mmm,' she murmured, dreamy-eyed. 'I could carry poppies and corn instead of the usual sort of bouquet, but

I don't think we'll be able to persuade Mollie to change her mind about the rose petals.'

And so it was arranged that the wedding would take place one Saturday in late September, the day after the village's harvest supper.

Pamela and Charles came back in August to reclaim their offspring, and not long after Henrietta was saying goodbye to the children she adored.

'But we'll see you soon, Aunt Henny,' said Mollie cheerily. 'You know, when I'm bridesmaid for you and Uncle Matthew.'

All the villagers had been delighted at Matthew and Henrietta's news, and the couple had found themselves flooded with offers for help with everything from the food to the flowers and the cake. The local seamstress had even offered to make Henrietta's dress. The days flew past in a flurry of organisation, and very soon it was the Friday before the wedding. Pamela, Charles and the children had arrived that morning, and as the last-minute details were sorted out, Henrietta heard all about the children's new home and school in Scandinavia.

'We love it there, but it's nice to be back here with you, Aunty Henny,' whispered Keiran, looking adorable as he tried on his pageboy outfit.

When they arrived at the village hall in the evening for the harvest supper, Henrietta observed the scene in amazement. Trestle tables with pristine white cloths on them were laden with fresh bread, every kind of cheese, fresh juices and pickles. And at one side of the room the farmers were standing behind smaller tables with huge joints of beef, pork, turkey and lamb sizzling in front of them and ready to carve.

'This is amazing,' she said, smiling at Matthew, who was now very much recovered from the accident.

'You haven't seen it all,' he told her. 'In the little room at the end there are huge apple pies and clotted cream, which is our traditional desert when we have a harvest supper.'

'Yummy!' Keiran cried, while Mollie clapped her hands and Henrietta hugged her beloved niece and nephew.

Kate was beaming at them from across the room with the smile that had been there ever since they'd told her they were to be married. It had followed the tears of joy she'd been shedding as she'd told Matthew, 'From the moment I saw Henrietta I knew that my prayers had been answered.'

Tomorrow she would be sitting proudly in a front pew of the village church, and so would Pamela, while Charles proudly escorted his sister-in-law down the aisle. The children would follow the bride, a bride dressed in cream brocade and carrying poppies and corn, going to meet her bridegroom. Mollie would be in a pretty long dress and scattering rose petals, and Keiran would be a cherubic pageboy.

Daniel had turned up for the harvest supper with a smiling young nurse pushing his wheelchair. It seemed that he'd got to know her while having the latest treatment for his paralysis.

While they were chatting to him the Martin family

arrived with a tall dark-haired youth that Henrietta knew must be their son.

Meriel had been to the surgery during the last week for the results of the blood tests on her swollen foot, which was now back to its normal size, and had been amazed to be told that it was gout.

'But I don't drink!' she'd protested, and Henrietta had smiled.

'You don't have to,' she'd told her. 'Drinkers do get it, but so do those who don't, I'm afraid.'

At the end of the consultation the vet's wife had said, 'Do you remember me telling you that our son was coming home? Well, he's due to arrive any day. I thought I'd better mention it.'

Henrietta had told Matthew and he'd said, 'It's all in the past, as far as I'm concerned. You've helped me to fight my demons. The hurt of what he did will never go away, but when I meet up with him I'll welcome him back and take it from there.'

She watched as he left Daniel's side, went across to the Martins and shook their son by the hand, which brought smiles of relief to all their faces.

When everyone was seated the vicar got to his feet and with his glance on the two doctors said, 'I'm sure that all of you know that tonight isn't the only big event of the weekend. Tomorrow we have the wedding of two highly respected members of our community, Matthew Cazalet, our dedicated doctor for many years, and Henrietta who came from city to village, also to look after our health, and found a very good reason for staying here in the man sitting beside her. To them both we say, every happiness.' As she listened, with Matthew's arm around her, Henrietta was reminded of what he'd said to her on the day she'd proposed to him in the hospital garden.

'It was a move in the right direction when you came to live in the village,' he'd said, and as they faced each other, with the promise of all the happiness to come in front of them, she knew just how right he had been. She'd changed her job so that she could look after Mollie and Keiran and had met the love of her life.

September had been a month of beginnings for Henrietta and Matthew, with their wedding in the old village church where every seat had been filled, and Henrietta moving into the house that she had helped decorate so willingly.

There had also been an ending, and Henrietta and Matthew had been sad to say goodbye to the children again the day after the wedding. They'd promised to write to each other all the time, and it was on a chilly November morning that Matthew found Henrietta in the kitchen, reading Mollie and Keiran's latest letter, written in a rainbow of bright colours. Seeing his wife's expression, he drew her into the comfort of his arms.

'I love them as if they're my own,' she told Matthew with a sad smile.

'Yes. I know you do,' he said tenderly, holding her close. 'What is happening to Mollie and Keiran is what happens to a lot of children in diplomats' families. But they'll come back soon, either permanently or on holiday, and with their parents *is* where they should be.'

He gave her a gentle kiss. 'The next time we see them *our* wonderful secret will be out in the open and they'll have a little cousin to love, won't they, Henrietta?'

'Yes,' she said softly as joy overcame sadness. 'A family of our own, Matthew.' He smiled at her, and there was all the love in the world in the eyes looking into hers.

MILLS & BOON®

0407/03b

Medical romance™

HIS RUNAWAY NURSE
by Meredith Webber

Twelve years after her sudden departure, Flynn can't believe his eyes when Majella Goldsworthy returns. She is nothing like the girl he once knew and now has a three-year-old daughter. Majella has come home to forge an independent life for herself and little Grace, but Flynn soon finds himself wondering if there could be room for one more in this very special family.

THE RESCUE DOCTOR'S BABY MIRACLE
by Dianne Drake

When Dr Gideon Merrill finds out Dr Lorna Preston is coming to film his search-and-rescue operation in a storm-devastated Brazilian village, everything about their failed marriage comes flooding back. But a night of passion changes everything and soon Gideon realises that he and Lorna have made a tiny miracle of their own...

EMERGENCY AT RIVERSIDE HOSPITAL
by Joanna Neil

Dr Kayleigh Byford has had enough of men – no matter how promising they start out, they always let her down. Her return to her home town has already had enough complications – the last thing she needs is another distraction in the form of Lewis McAllister, her seriously gorgeous boss at Riverside A&E!

On sale 4th May 2007

Available at WHSmith, Tesco, ASDA, and all good bookshops

www.millsandboon.co.uk

4 FREE

BOOKS AND A SURPRISE GIFT!

We would like to take this opportunity to thank you for reading this Mills & Boon® book by offering you the chance to take FOUR more specially selected titles from the Medical Romance™ series absolutely FREE! We're also making this offer to introduce you to the benefits of the Mills & Boon® Reader Service™—

- ★ FREE home delivery
- ★ FREE gifts and competitions
- ★ FREE monthly Newsletter
- ★ Exclusive Reader Service offers
- ★ Books available before they're in the shops

Accepting these FREE books and gift places you under no obligation to buy, you may cancel at any time, even after receiving your free shipment. Simply complete your details below and return the entire page to the address below. You don't even need a stamp!

YES! Please send me 4 free Medical Romance books and a surprise gift. I understand that unless you hear from me, I will receive 6 superb new titles every month for just £2.89 each, postage and packing free. I am under no obligation to purchase any books and may cancel my subscription at any time. The free books and gift will be mine to keep in any case.

M7ZED

Ms/Mrs/Miss/Mr ....Initials ....
BLOCK CAPITALS PLEASE
Surname ....
Address ....

....
....Postcode...

Send this whole page to:
UK: FREEPOST CN81, Croydon, CR9 3WZ